# Victory Over Abu Derya

# Victory Over Abu Derya

The Quest for Pearls in the Arabian Gulf

Written and illustrated by

Mohammed Ali

دار بلومزبري– مؤسسة قطر للنشر
BLOOMSBURY
QATAR FOUNDATION
PUBLISHING

مؤسسة قطر
Qatar Foundation

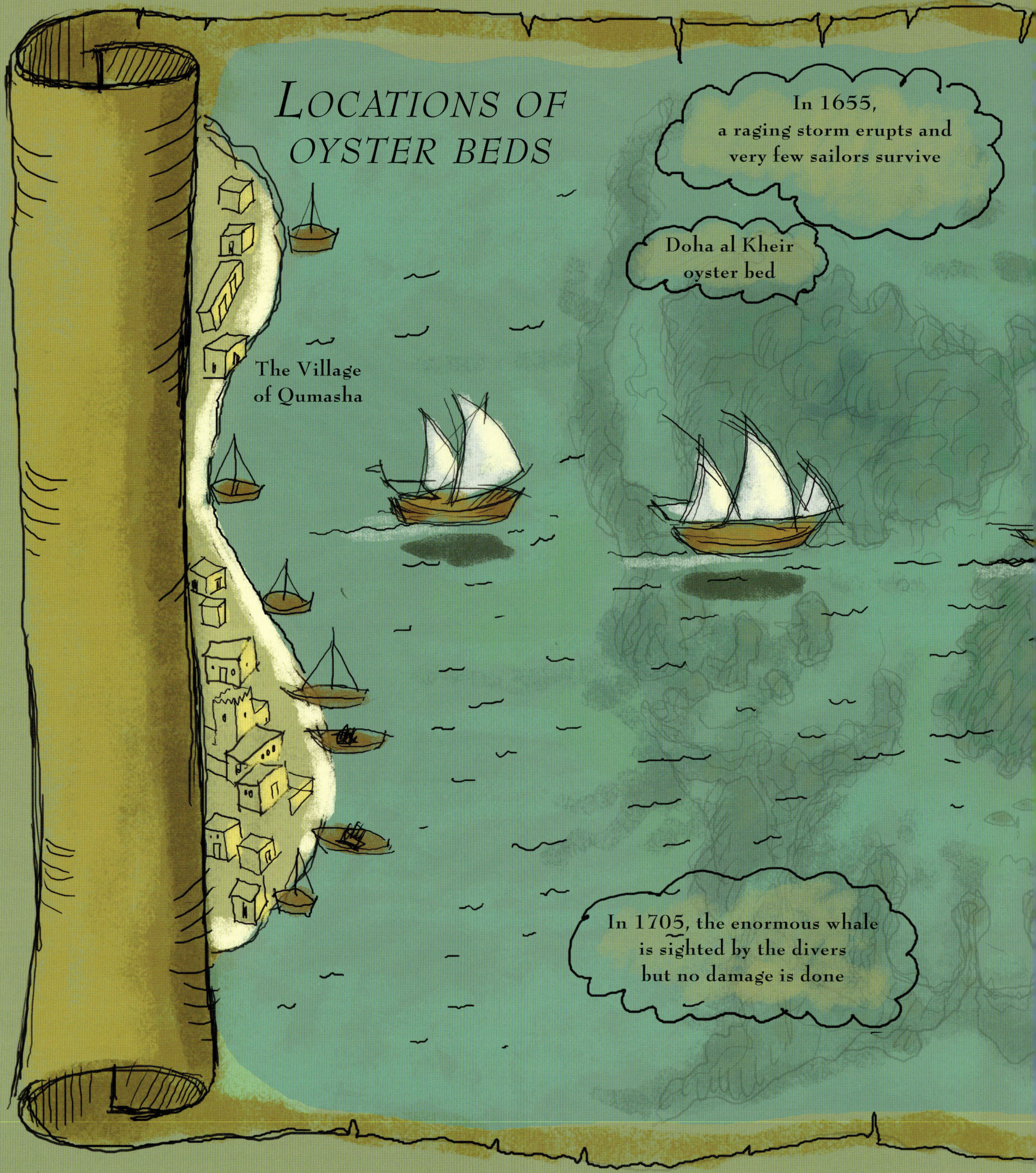
LOCATIONS OF OYSTER BEDS
In 1655, a raging storm erupts and very few sailors survive
Doha al Kheir oyster bed
The Village of Qumasha
In 1705, the enormous whale is sighted by the divers but no damage is done

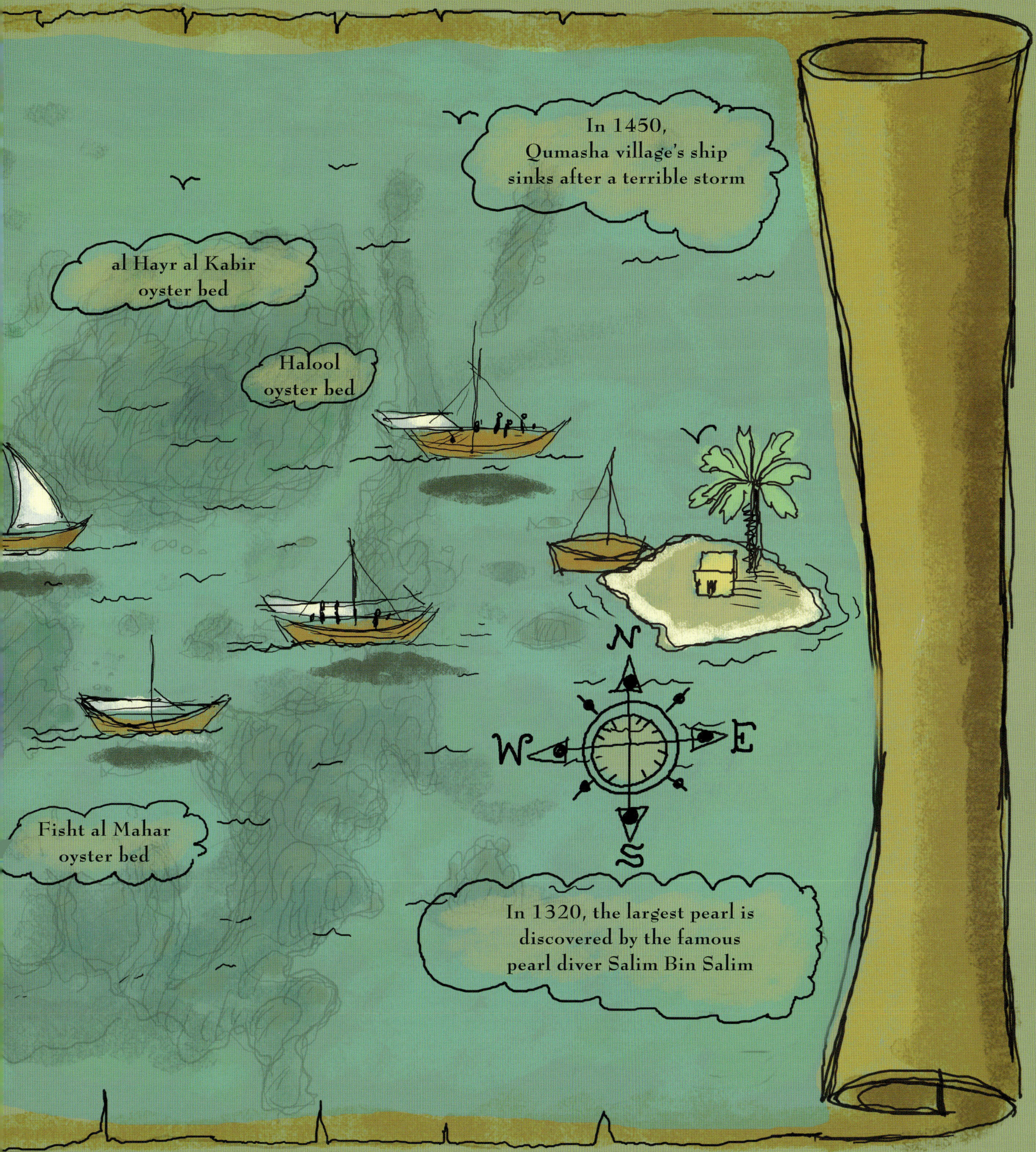
In 1450,
Qumasha village's ship
sinks after a terrible storm
al Hayr al Kabir
oyster bed
Halool
oyster bed
N
W
E
S
Fisht al Mahar
oyster bed
In 1320, the largest pearl is
discovered by the famous
pearl diver Salim Bin Salim

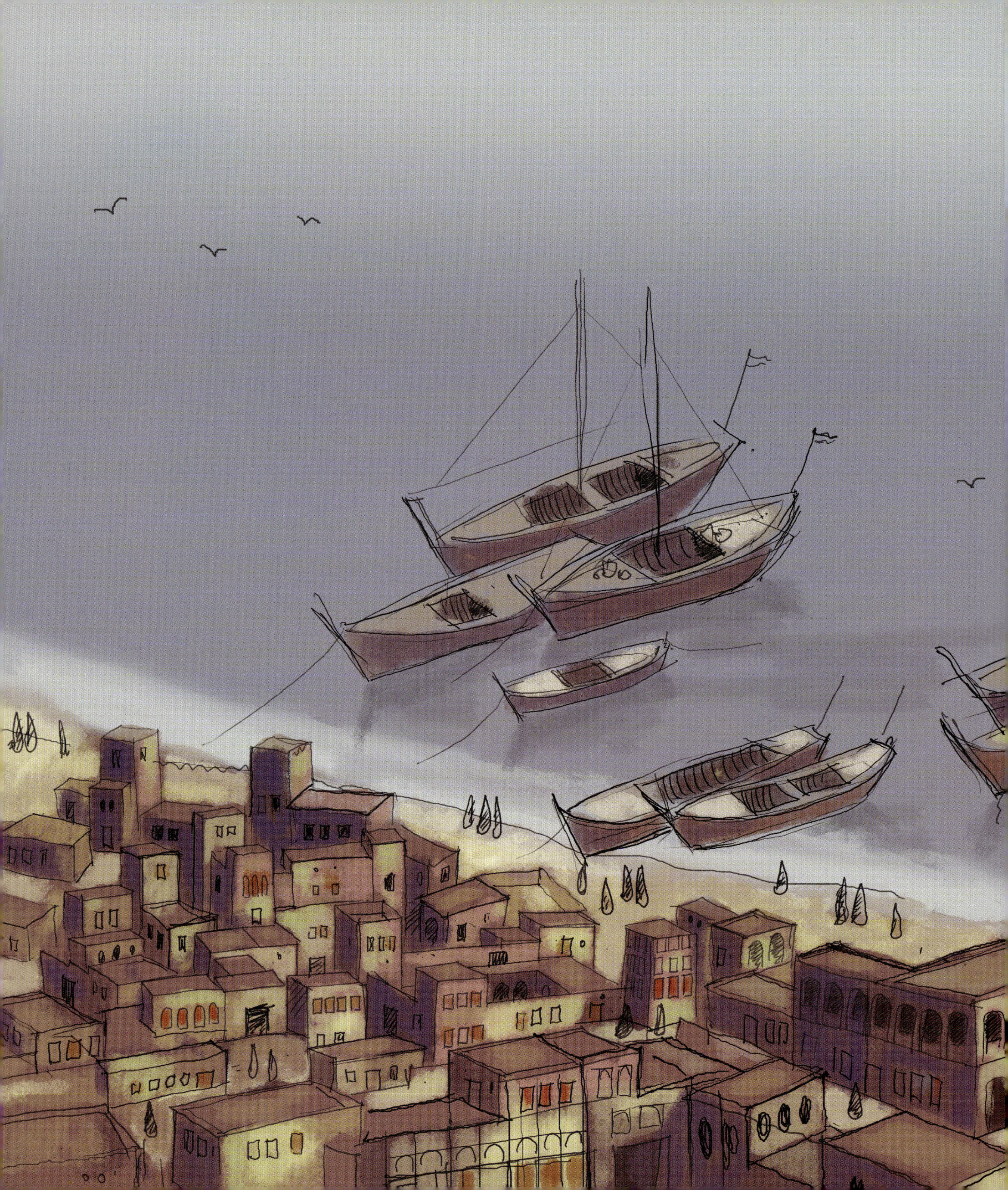

## *Introduction*

For thousands of years, from the time of the ancient Assyrians and Sumerians, the people of the Gulf waged a fierce, relentless struggle to capture precious pearls from the seabed. Their opponent was Abu Derya, the legendary guard of the Kingdom of the Seas, who used all the forces at his disposal to protect his treasures.

This story is one of many that might have taken place on the coast of the Arabian Gulf, over two hundred years ago.

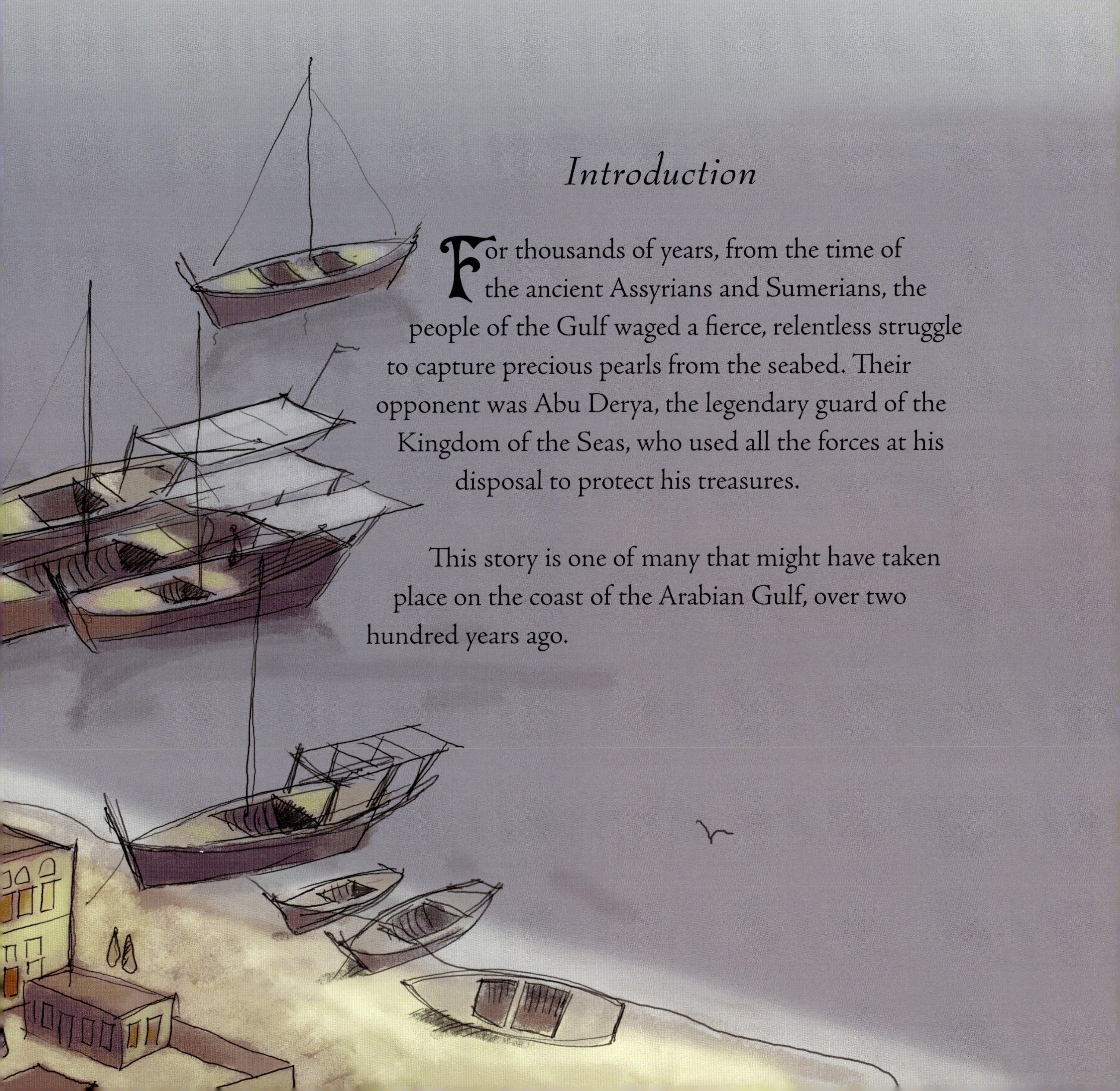

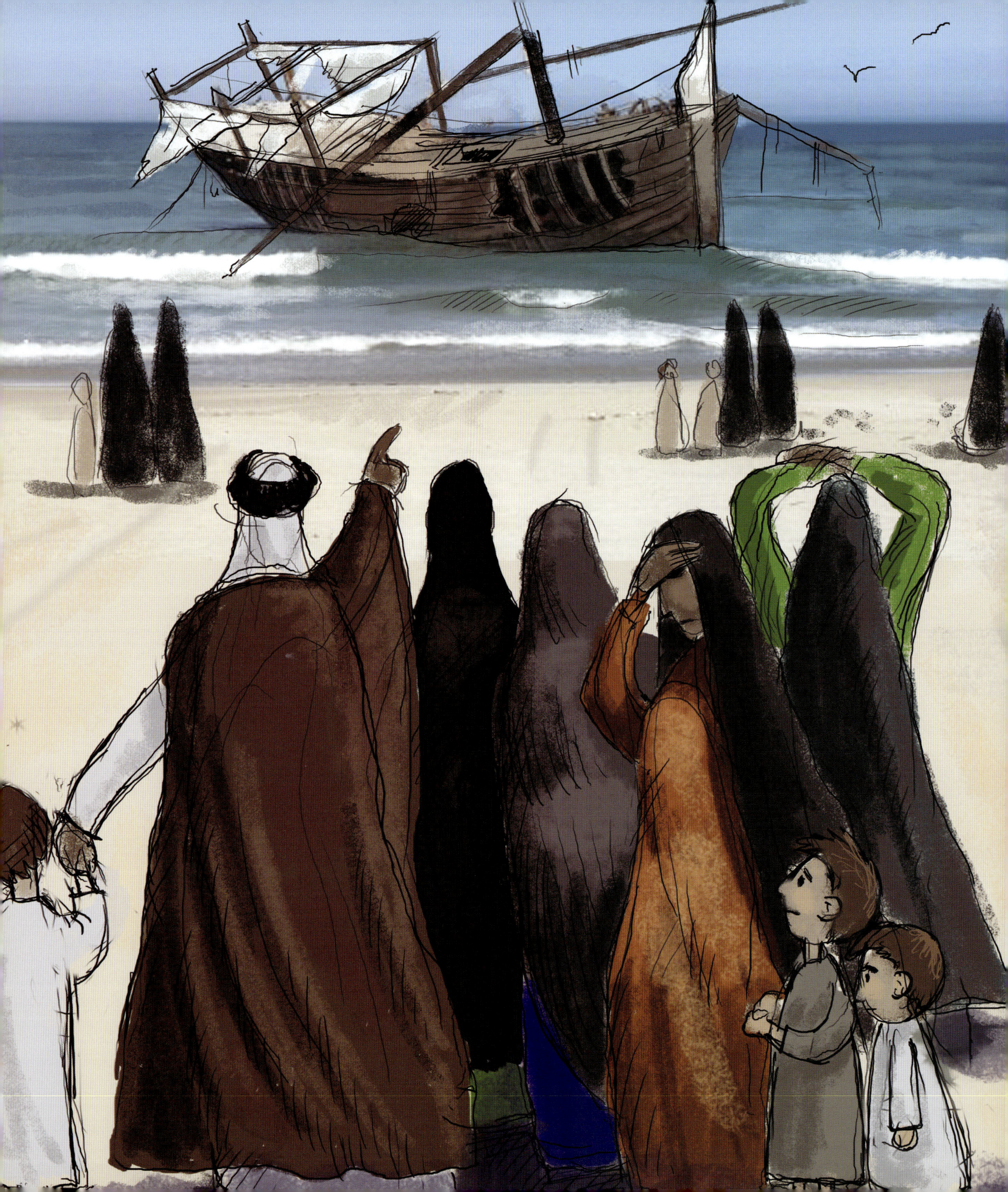

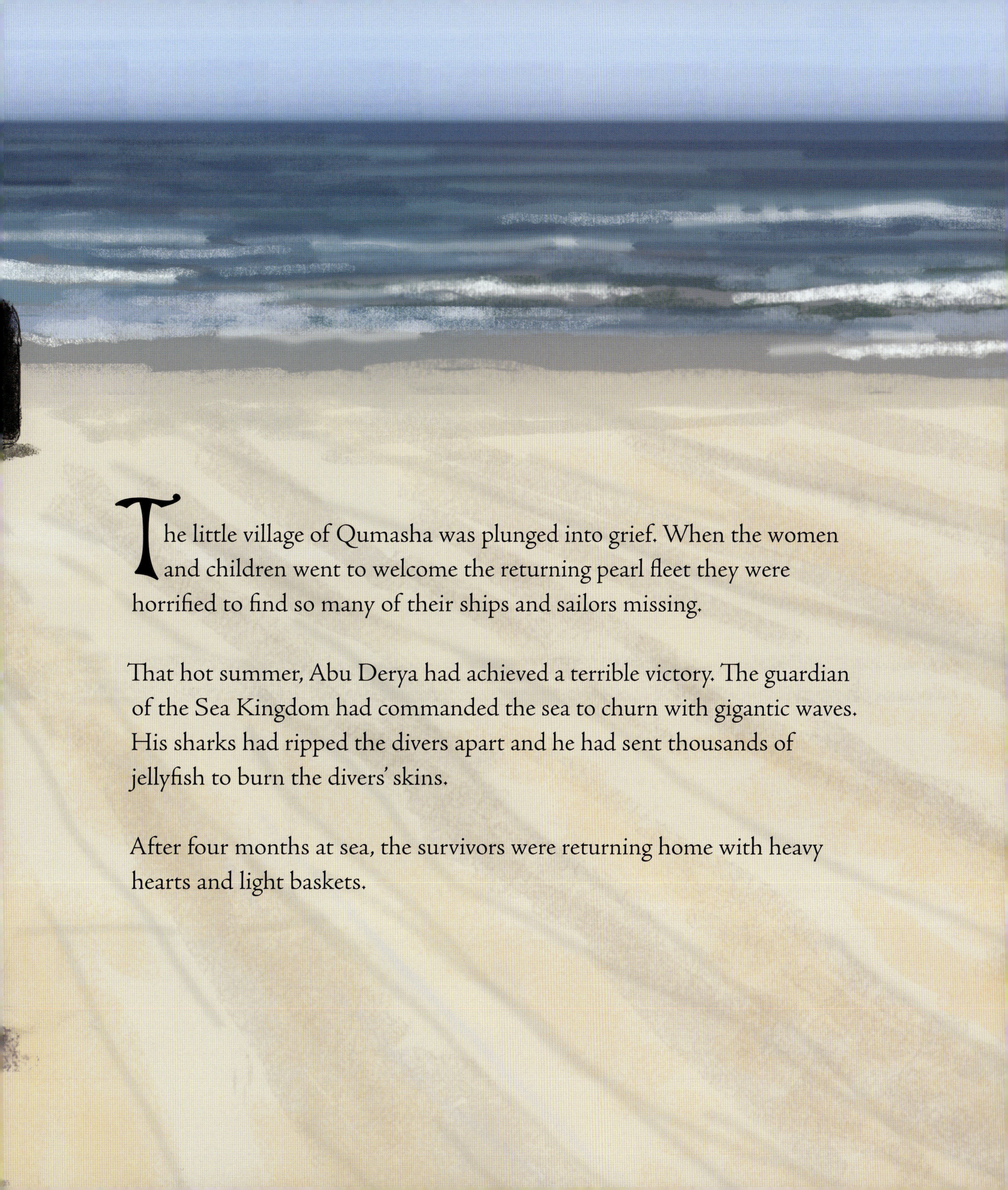

The little village of Qumasha was plunged into grief. When the women and children went to welcome the returning pearl fleet they were horrified to find so many of their ships and sailors missing.

That hot summer, Abu Derya had achieved a terrible victory. The guardian of the Sea Kingdom had commanded the sea to churn with gigantic waves. His sharks had ripped the divers apart and he had sent thousands of jellyfish to burn the divers' skins.

After four months at sea, the survivors were returning home with heavy hearts and light baskets.

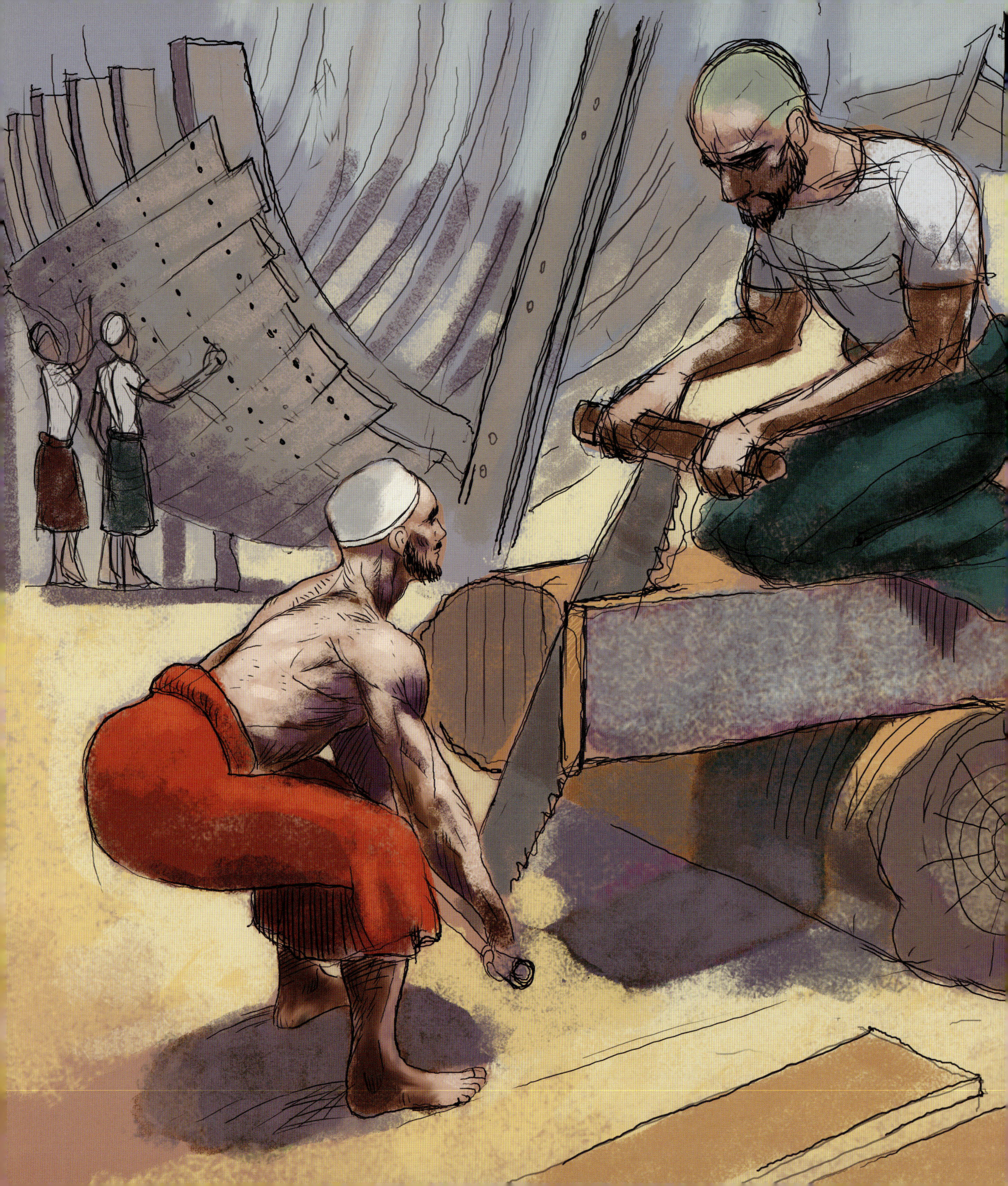

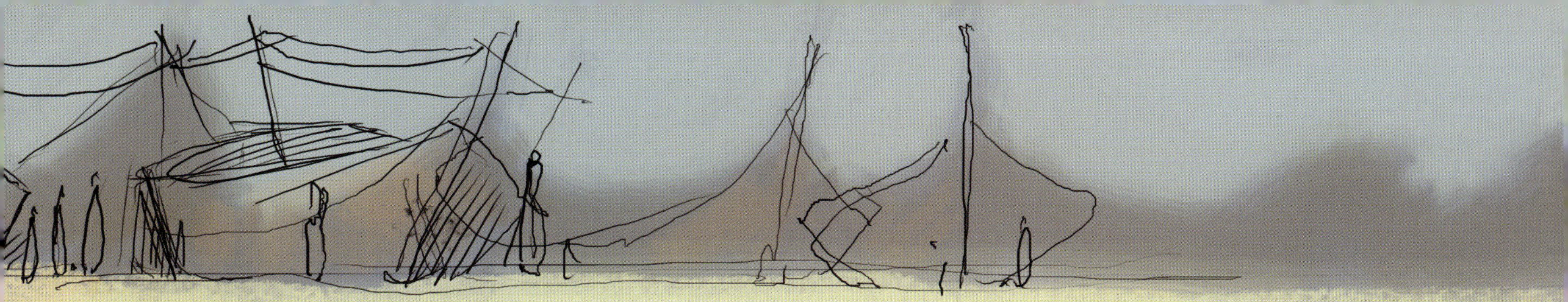

The following year, the people of the village prepared themselves thoroughly. They brought skilful boatbuilders and expensive teakwood from India. They built new boats and ships that could carry up to a hundred divers. The largest of the ships had three sails, stretched on masts made from wood that could withstand the strongest storms.

The village did not rest for a moment. The weavers wove sails from the finest cotton, the blacksmiths made new nails, and the divers themselves made new ropes. All were determined to win the struggle against the Kingdom of the Seas and its fearsome guard, Abu Derya.

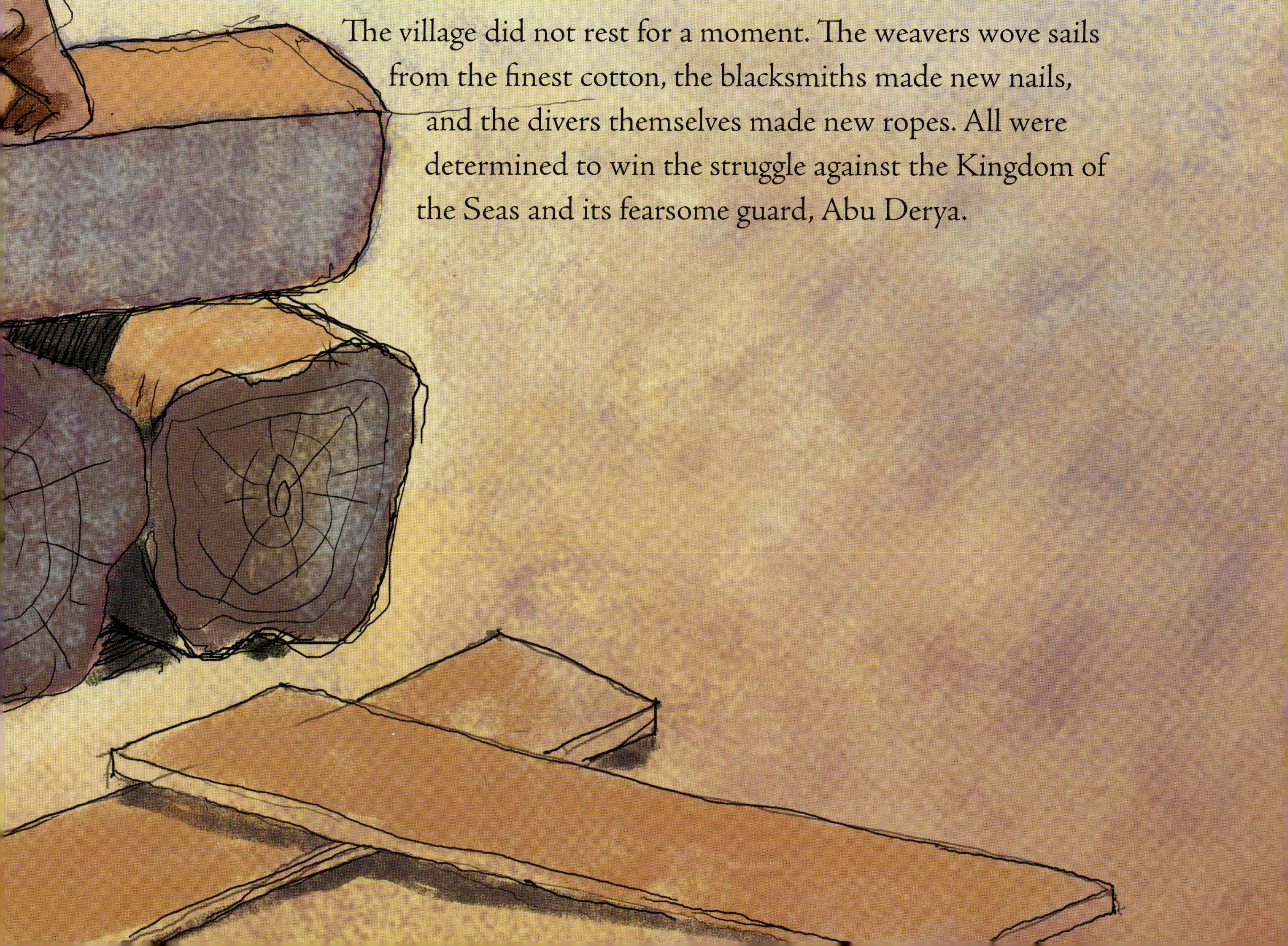

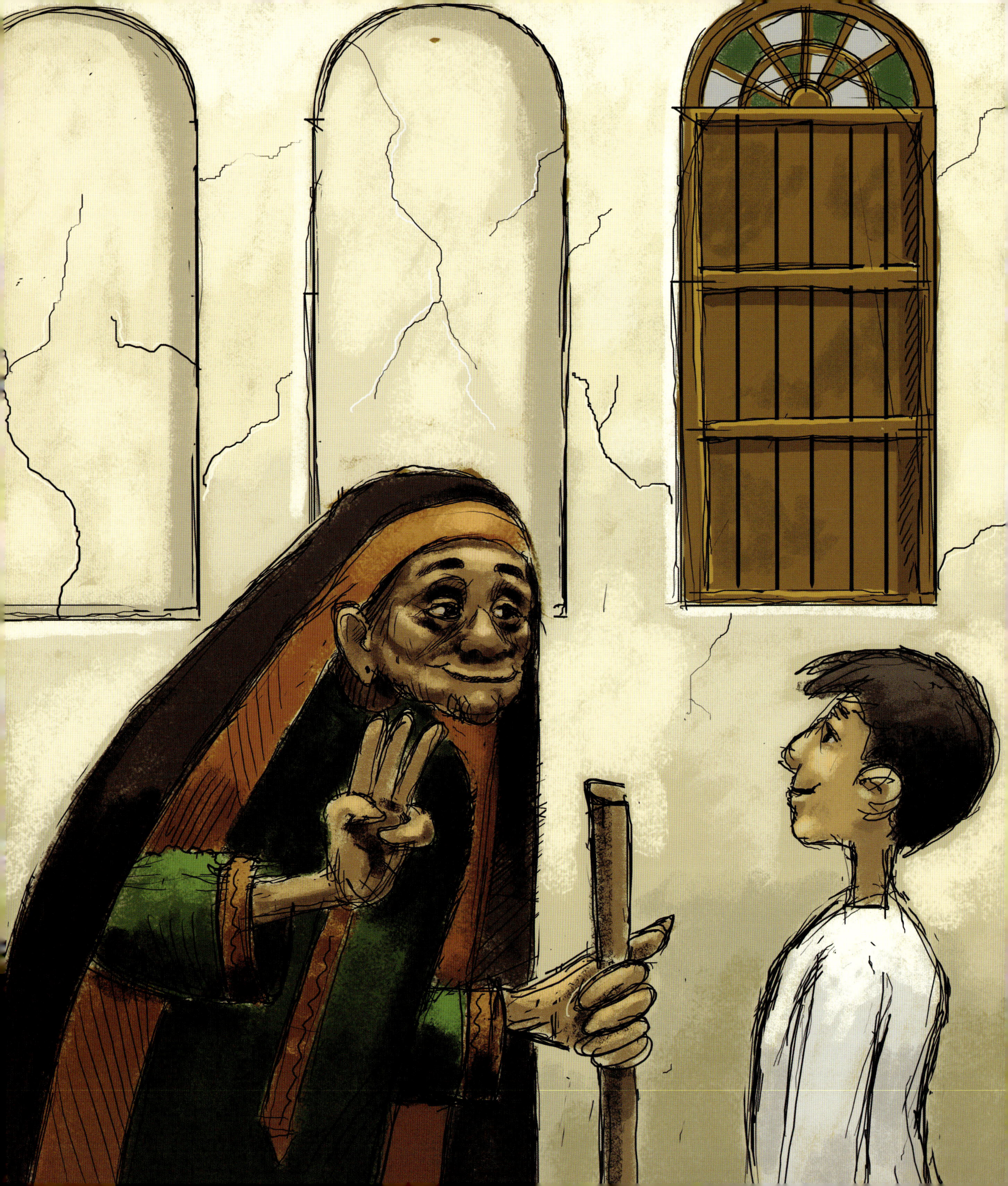

The villagers' excitement grew. The oldest lady of the village had had the same dream for three nights in a row. In the dream, her grandson Rashid's hand was filled with huge pearls and Abu Derya was standing behind him, weeping bitterly over the defeat that he had suffered.

"You must travel on this voyage," Rashid's grandmother told him with a smile. "The signs are promising!"

Although Rashid was very happy at the idea of making his first voyage, he was also worried. He knew the dangers that faced the men at sea.

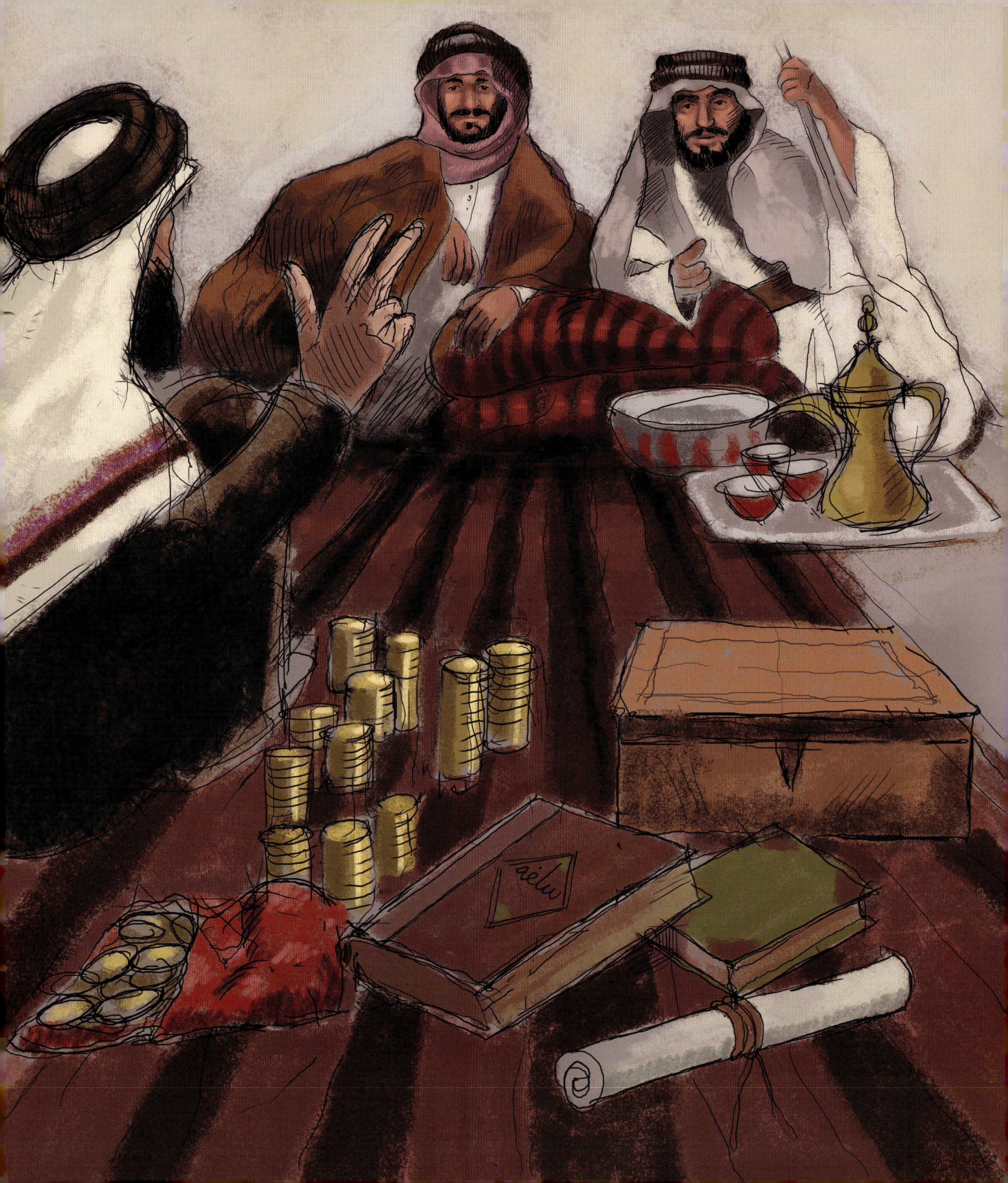

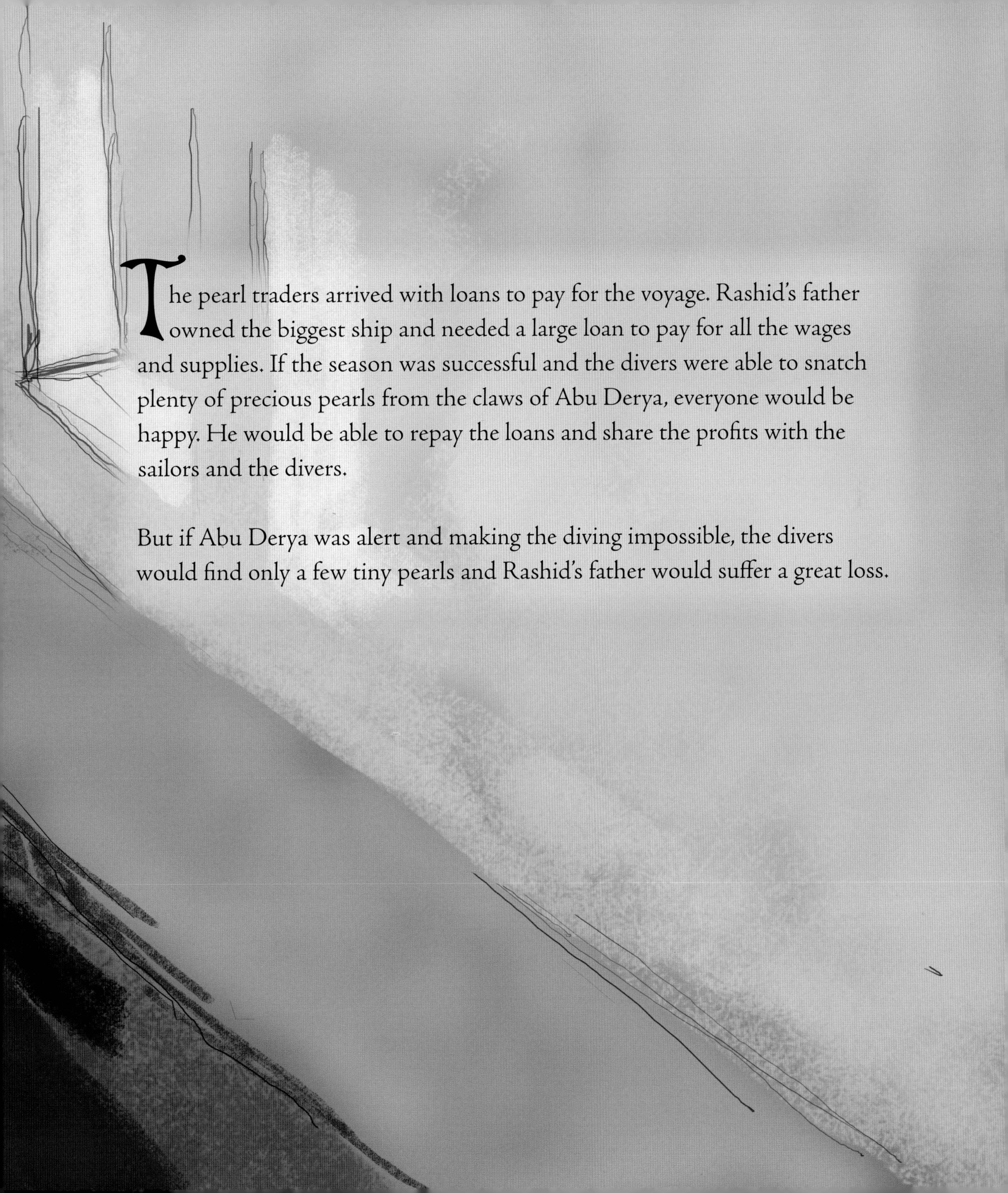

The pearl traders arrived with loans to pay for the voyage. Rashid's father owned the biggest ship and needed a large loan to pay for all the wages and supplies. If the season was successful and the divers were able to snatch plenty of precious pearls from the claws of Abu Derya, everyone would be happy. He would be able to repay the loans and share the profits with the sailors and the divers.

But if Abu Derya was alert and making the diving impossible, the divers would find only a few tiny pearls and Rashid's father would suffer a great loss.

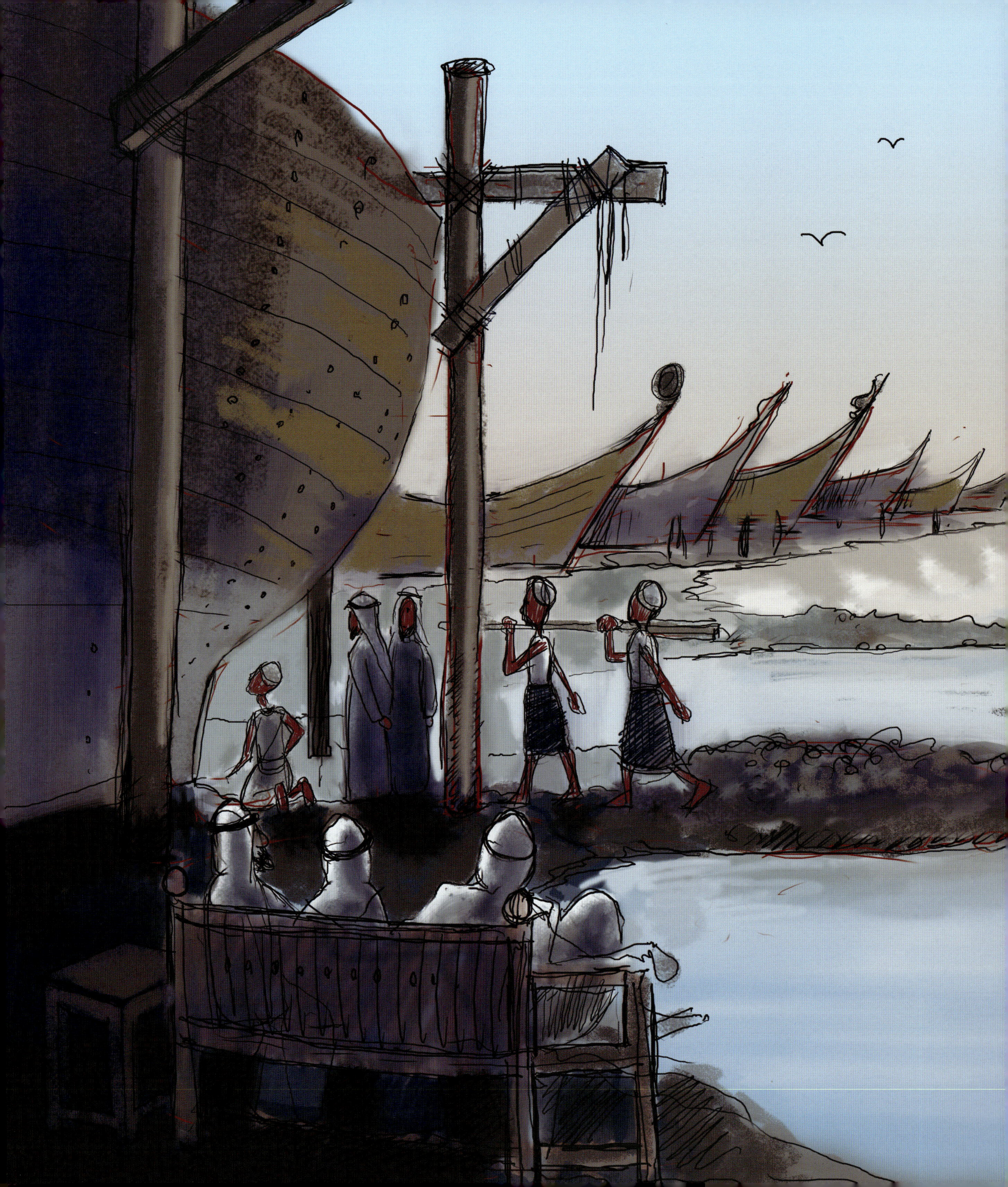

Now Rashid's father and the other ship-owners chose the members of their crews. Each ship needed a captain, a first mate, divers, rope-holders and young apprentices who would learn the ways of pearl diving.

Rashid's father's ship would carry the emir of the fleet, who would lead the ships of Qumasha in their confrontation with Abu Derya.

Rashid would also be traveling on his father's ship. He was given the task of collecting the stones that the divers would tie to their legs to help them sink quickly to the bottom of the sea.

It was June, when the summer winds blew loud and hot over the land, stirring up the sands and the sea, making great waves and turning the water murky. This was when the oysters were ready and when the people of Qumasha set out for their latest battle with the sea. It was the great embarkation. The whole village came to say farewell to their men, their most precious possession, who were departing on a journey of four months.

The village women, the elderly and the children started to sing songs. Although the words were happy and the rhythms joyful, their sad voices could not conceal their worries. Some raised their hands to the heavens, praying to all-providing, merciful God to fulfil their hopes, to bring victory over Abu Derya and to return their men safely.

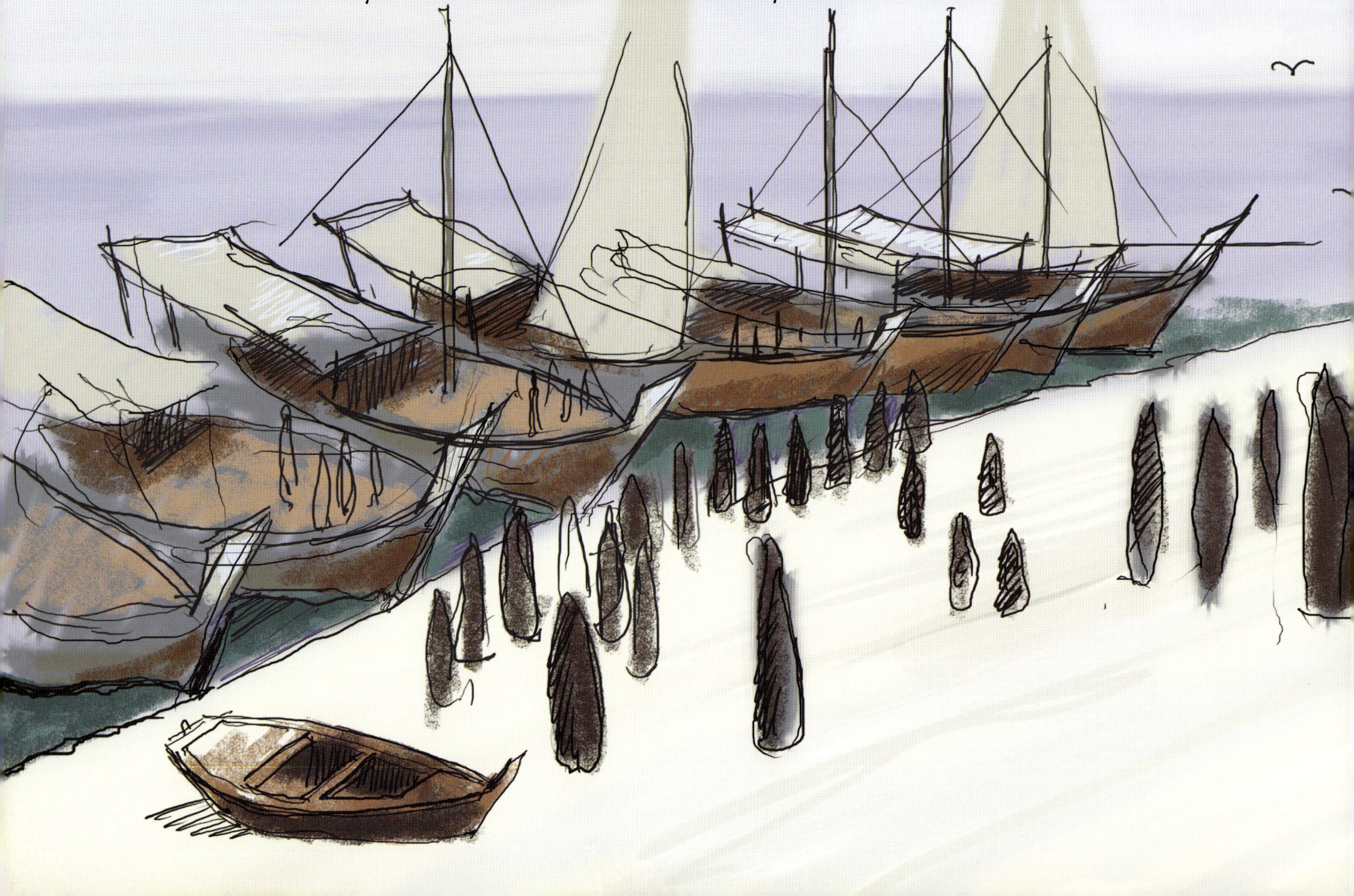

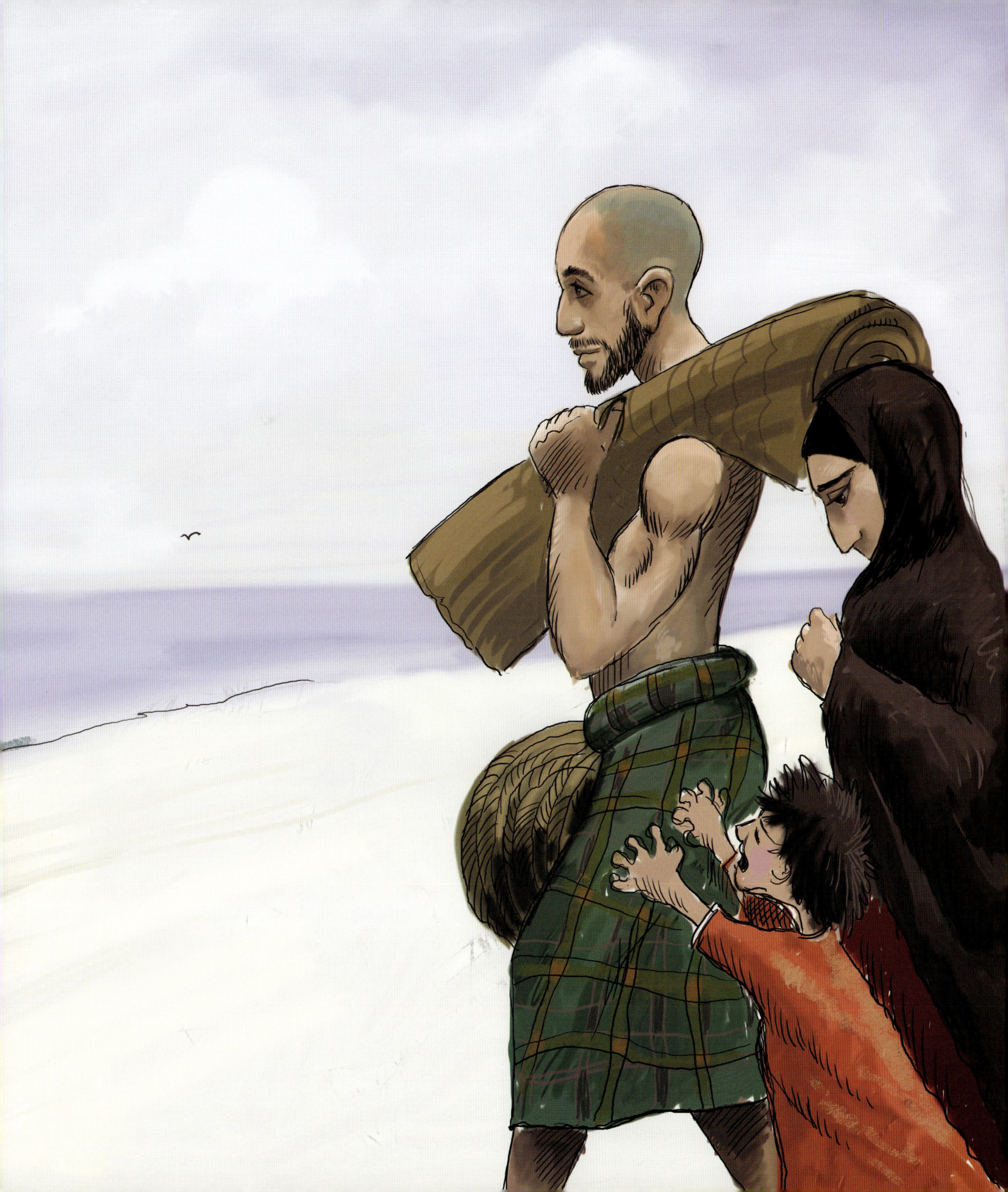

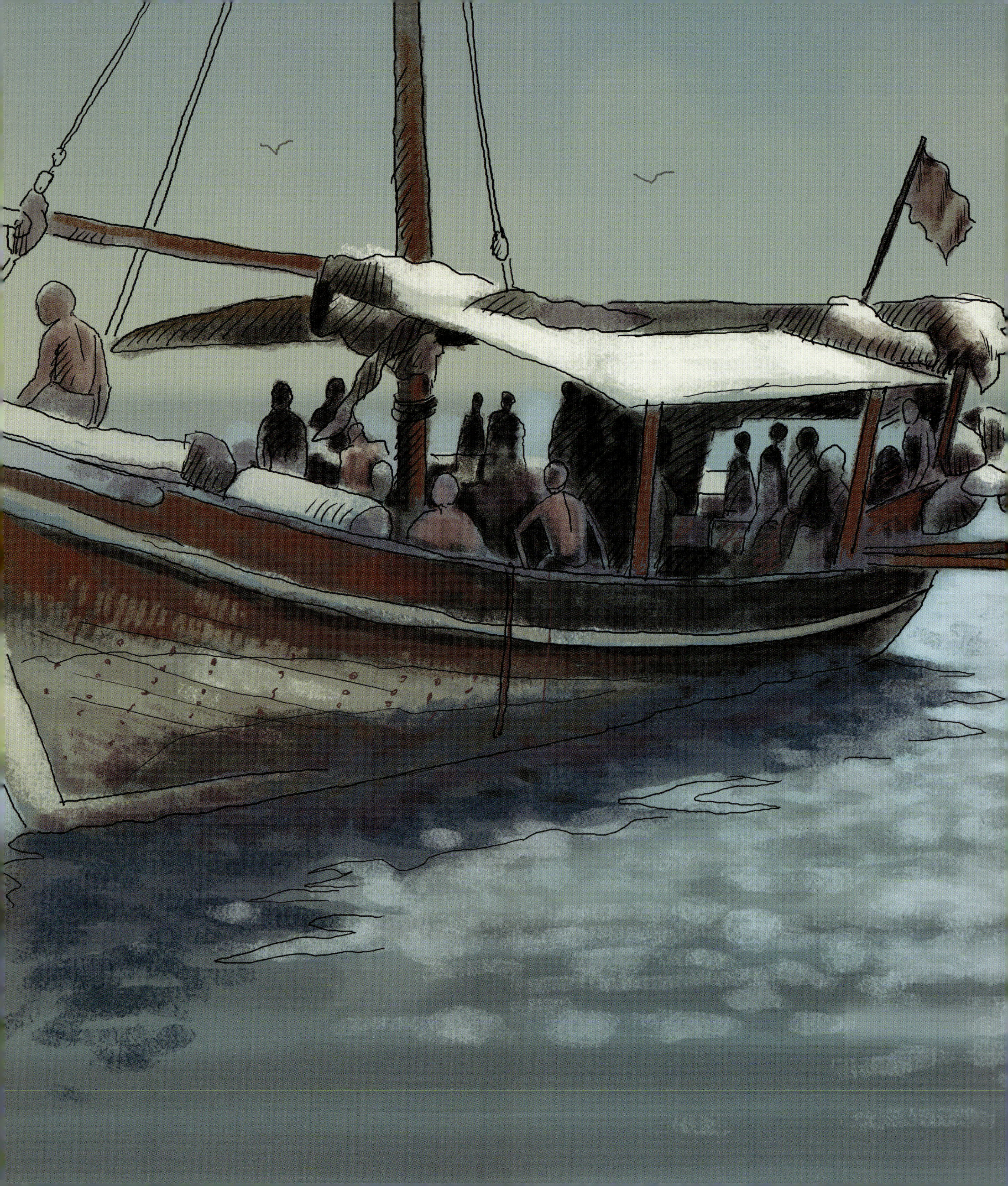

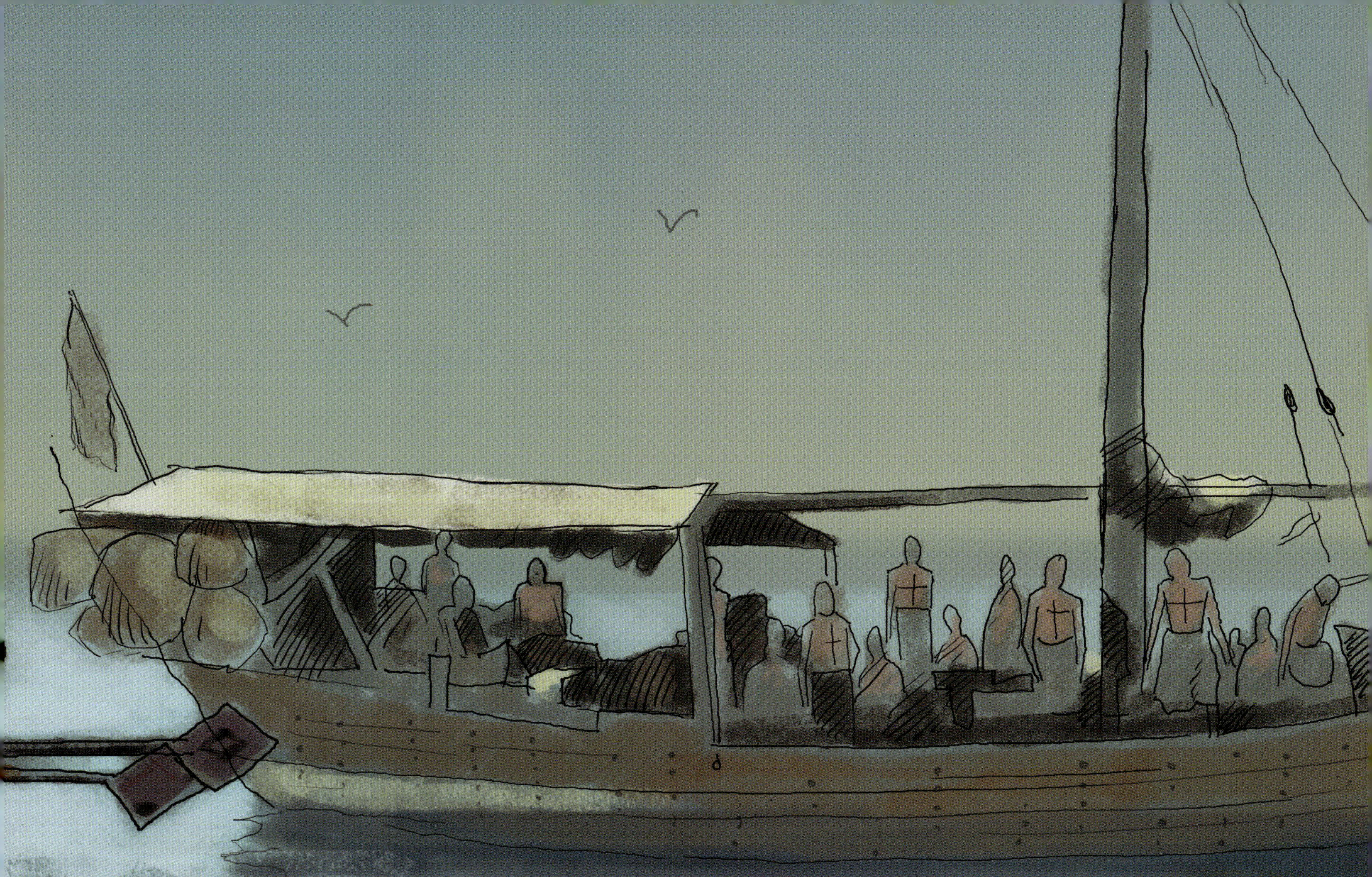

Just before the break of dawn the emir of Qumasha fired the ship's cannon. The shot echoed across the sea, announcing the start of the voyage. The other ships raised their anchors and spread their sails. The ships' chanters, who accompanied the sailors on all their voyages, began to sing and pray to God for a prosperous season. Their heart-rending tunes were echoed by the sailors. It was the last scene that the village of Qumasha witnessed before the ships disappeared over the horizon of the turquoise sea.

The emir of Qumasha had chosen the field of battle. The ships were heading towards the oyster beds located between the islands of Bahrain and Delma, around the Qatari peninsula.

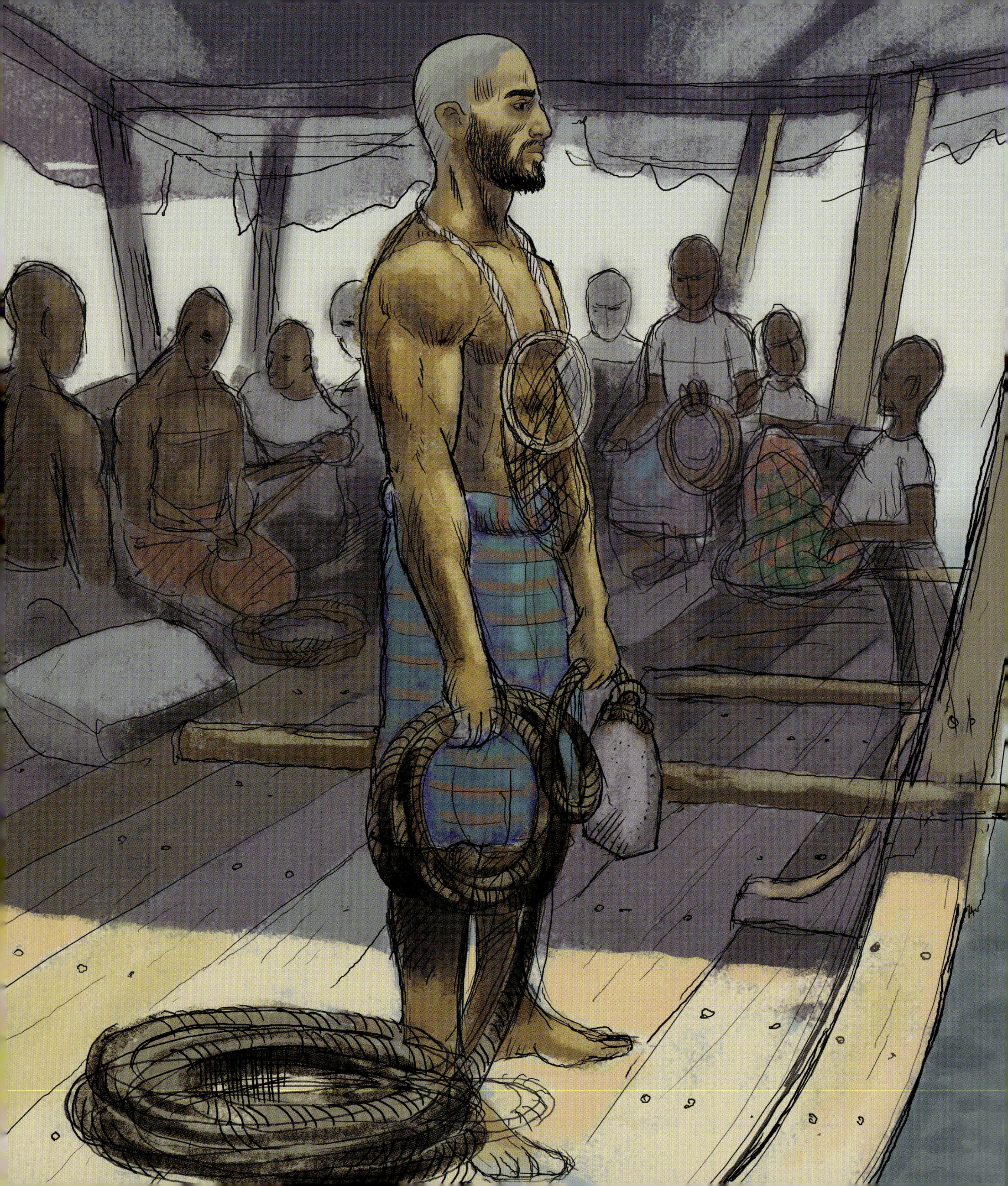

When the ships reached their destination, they lowered their stone anchors and the divers started to sing:

*Blessed be our descent, blessed be our home,*
*Bless the oysters and the oyster beds.*
*Our hopes lie in the dive to come*
*And in God who provides.*

The struggle with the cruel world was about to begin again. In this desolate place Abu Derya had prepared the men's defeat. The sharks were ready and ravenous, as well as lionfish, jellyfish, and other terrible sea creatures. But the glimmer of the pearls and the dream of victory in the imaginations of the divers overcame any fear or hesitation. For them, this glimmer represented the transition from poverty to riches.

The divers called upon God before taking up their positions and jumping into the sea with the baskets around their necks and the clips on their noses. Every rope-holder held his diver's rope firmly and waited to hear the captain's signal – a loud clear 'Bismillah' that rang through the air.

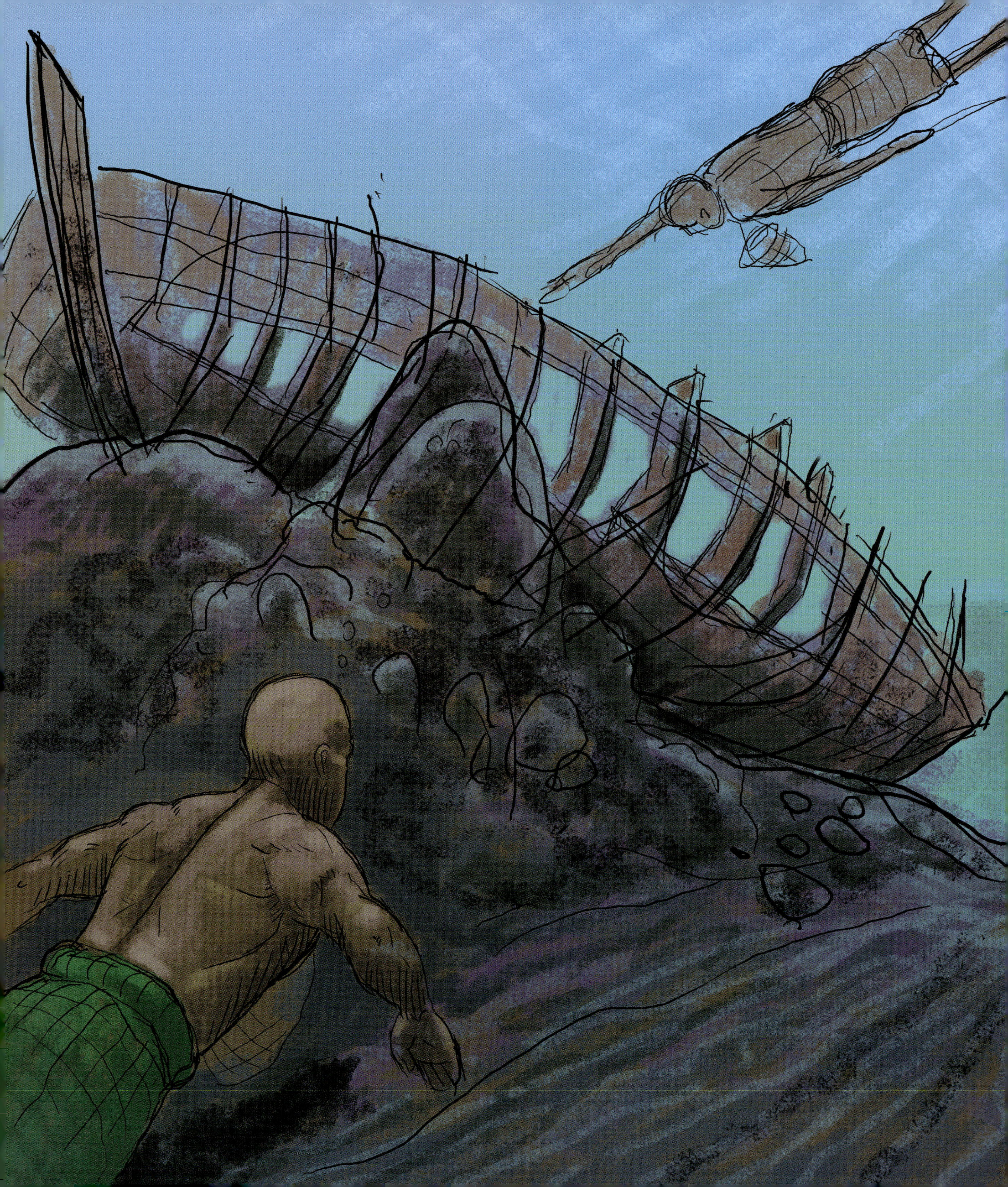

With the weights tied to their legs, the divers reached the bottom of the sea in just a few seconds. For up to a minute and a half they searched for oysters. Whenever a diver found an oyster he put it in the basket until he felt that the basket could not hold any more – then he tugged the rope and the rope-holder immediately pulled the diver up. At the surface the diver took a deep breath and rested for a few moments, while the rope-holder took the basket of oysters and emptied it onto the deck. After the diver had recovered, he took a deep breath and allowed the weights on his leg to pull him back down.

The piles of oysters on the decks of the ships grew larger, but no-one attempted to open the precious oysters yet. This was always left until the end of the voyage.

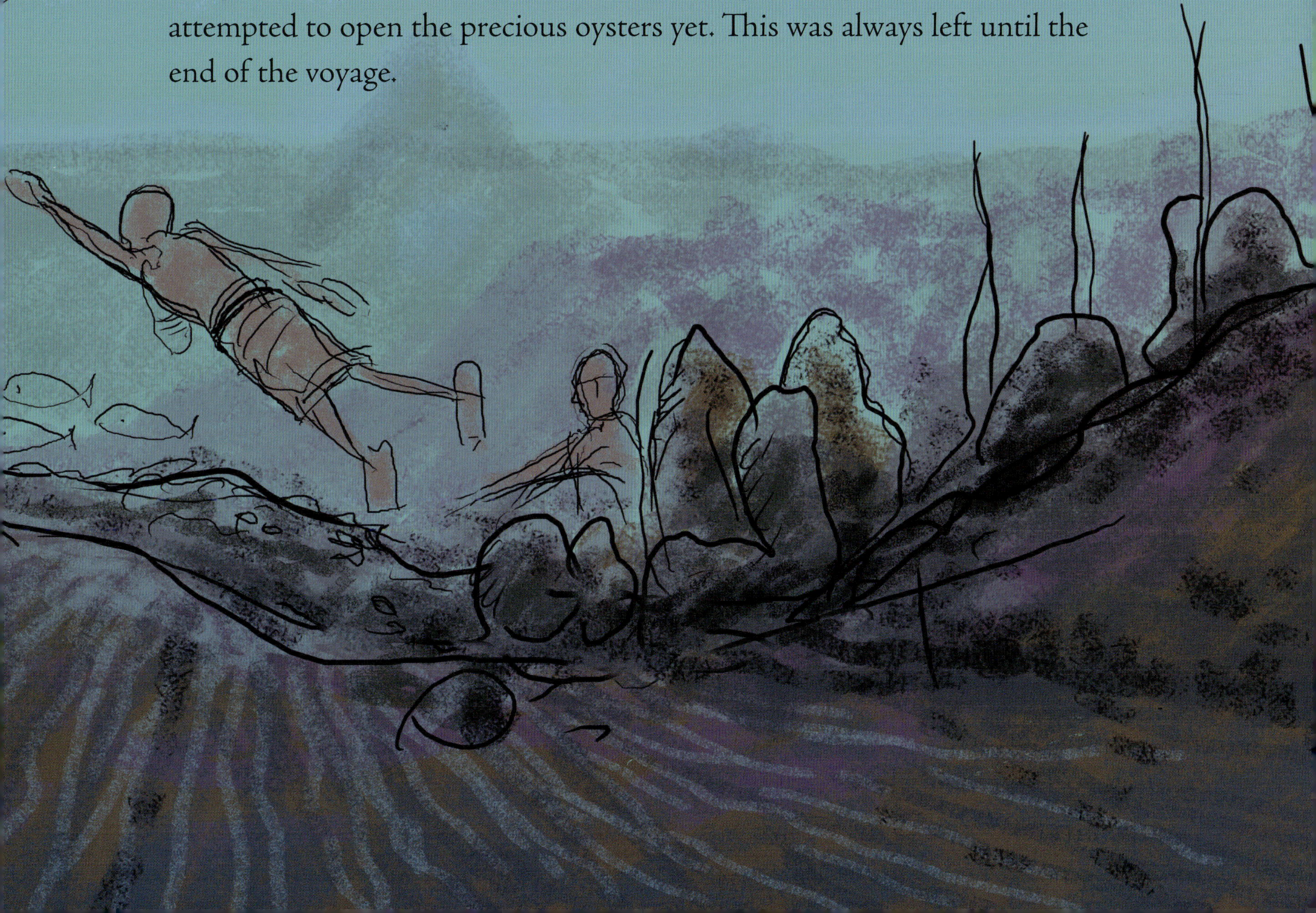

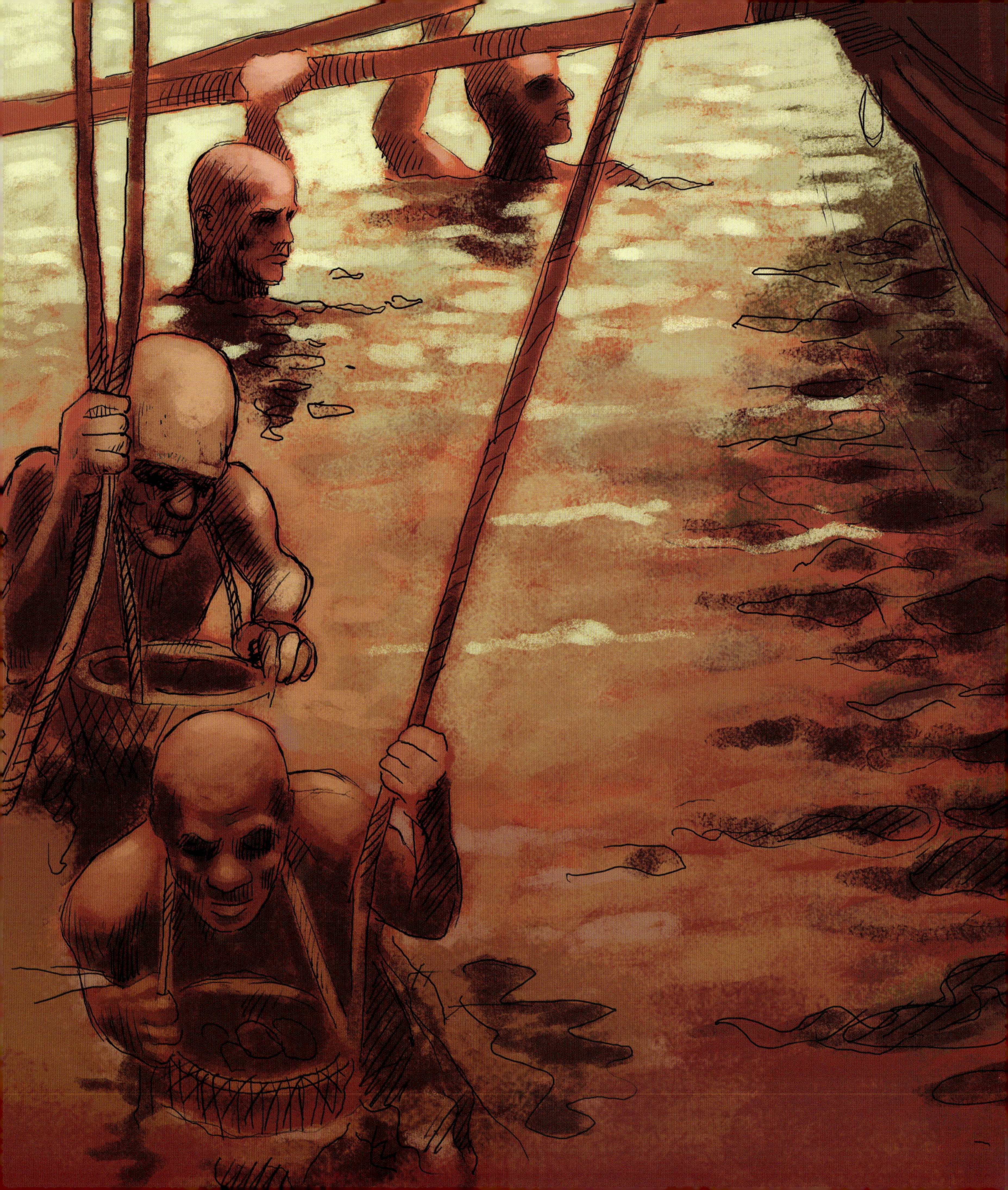

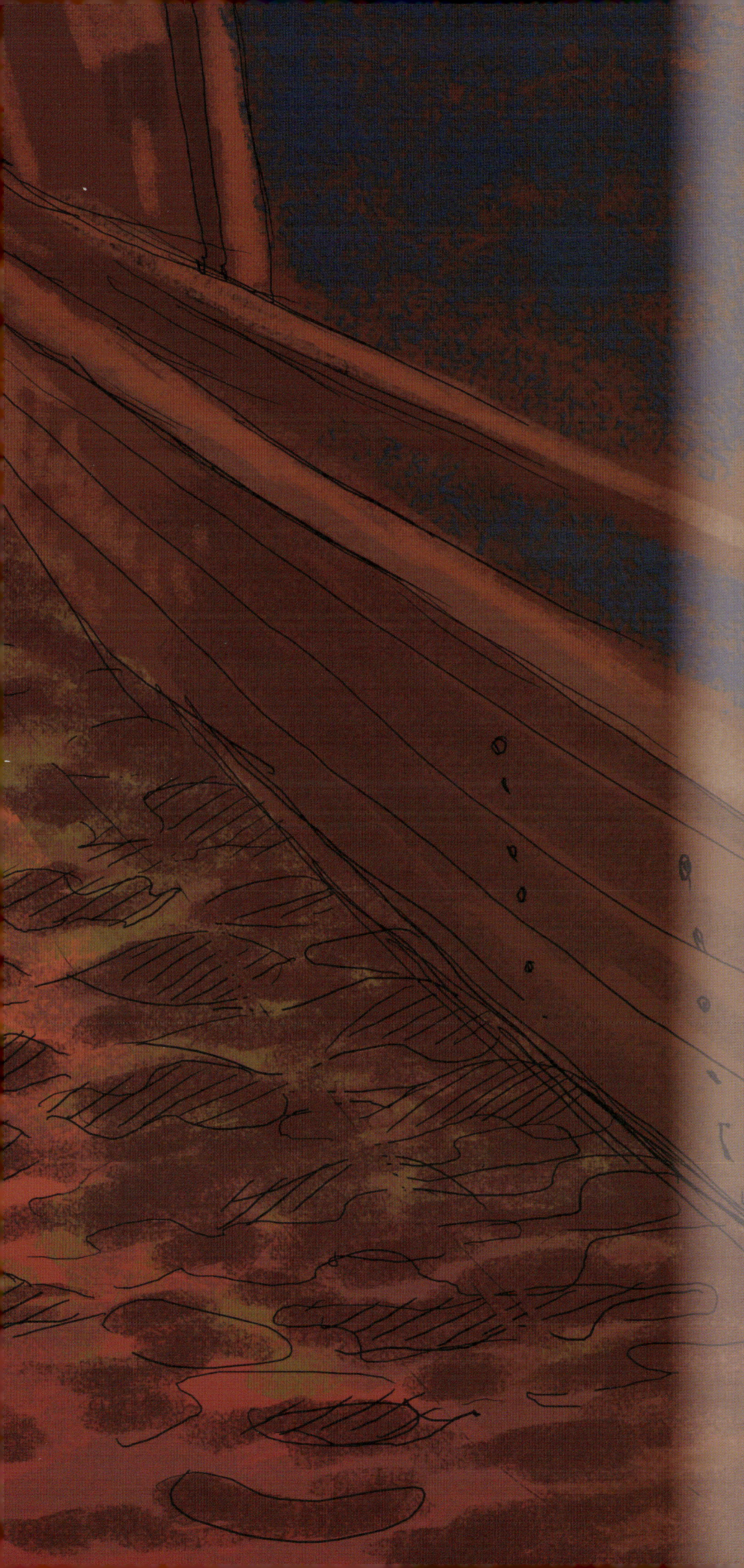

By the time the sun had set at the end of the first day, everyone on the ship was exhausted. It was time for food. The cooks prepared the rice and grilled the fish that was a precious reward for everyone, fuelling the divers for the hard day that would come with the new dawn. Rashid had the task of helping to prepare the food as well as making sure the ropes and equipment were all in place for the next day.

As soon as the evening prayer was called they all gathered to thank God for everything they had gained that day. After the prayer, each had his own private moment with God, the provider and owner of all, who gives prosperity at all times and brings victory and hope to whoever offers Him supplication.

The exhausted bodies slept deeply, lying on the ropes and shells as if they were made of the softest cotton.

At the first sign of dawn, an hour before sunrise, the first mate of the emir's ship stamped on the deck with the familiar rhythm that all the sailors understood. This was the moment to wake up and prepare for a new day. For Rashid it felt as if he had only had a few minutes of sleep, but now he had to help with the breakfast preparations.

The muezzin announced the dawn prayer. The divers lined up behind their fellow crew members and performed the prayer. By now the cook had prepared the breakfast – a pot of coffee with a strong smell of cardamom, and a few dates.

Fully awake, everyone returned to their places – the divers in the sea, the men holding their ropes, all awaiting the captain's signal. And so began another day's battle with the sea.

The captain had only one thing on his mind, to harvest as many oysters as possible before his supply of food and water ran out, forcing him to turn back.

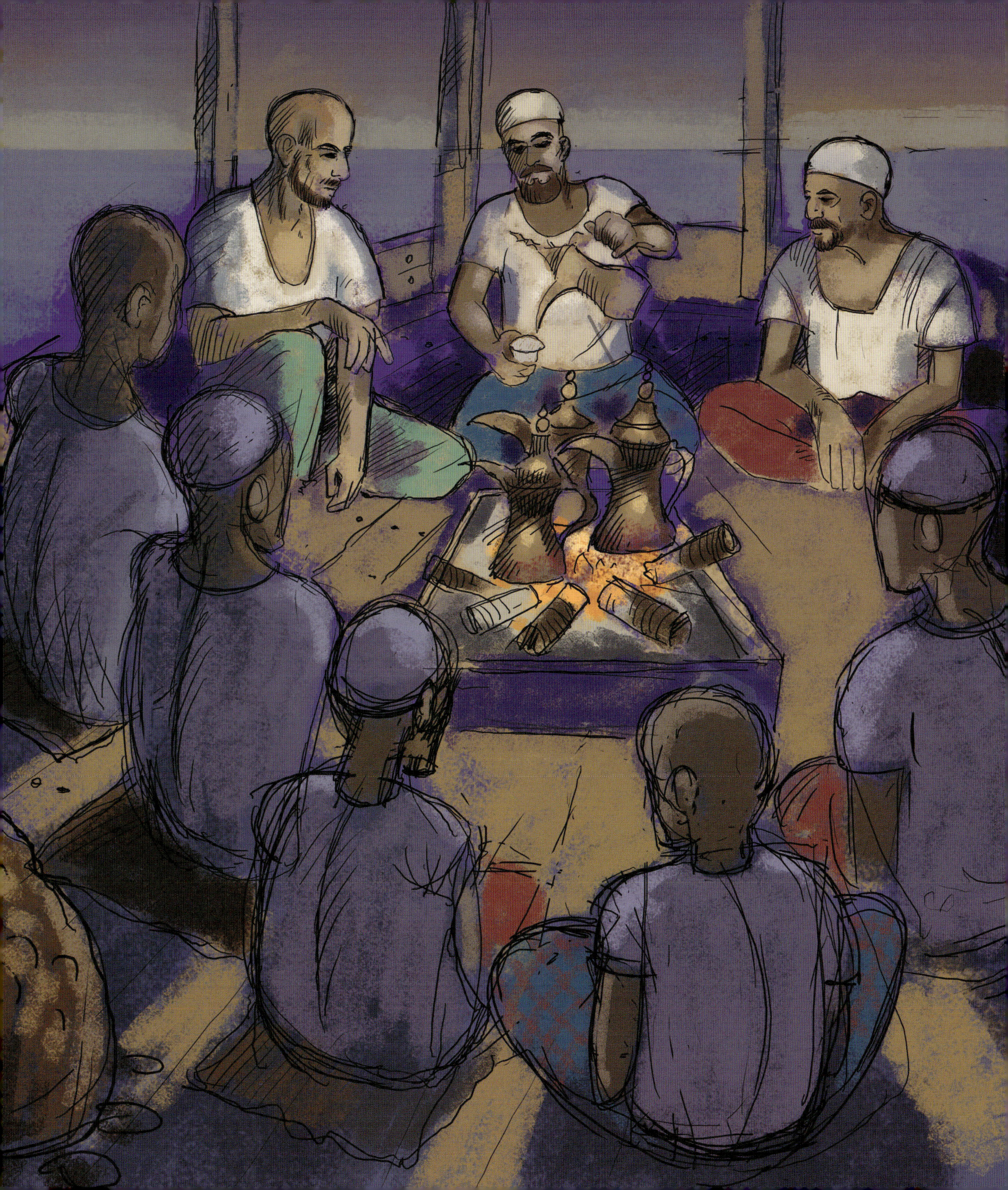

In the middle of the day, while the divers were busy at the bottom of the sea, a huge whale suddenly appeared, casting a shadow that stretched across the sea. Abu Derya had sent his messengers the crabs to the deepest farthest seas to call upon the sea's mightiest creature, the sperm whale, to help defeat his enemies.

The first to see the whale was Rashid, who shouted as loudly as possible to warn the crew. The rope-holders started frantically to pull the divers from the bottom of the sea with all their strength but the whale, which was almost as big as the ship, rushed through the water towards them. The crew members gathered on deck and started banging their cooking utensils and drums to scare the whale away. Some of the men began supplications to God.

The whale thrashed the water, sending huge waves crashing into the ship. Its tail struck the hull, which shattered with a deafening crack and sent hundreds of sharp wooden pieces flying into the air. Seawater began to enter the ship.

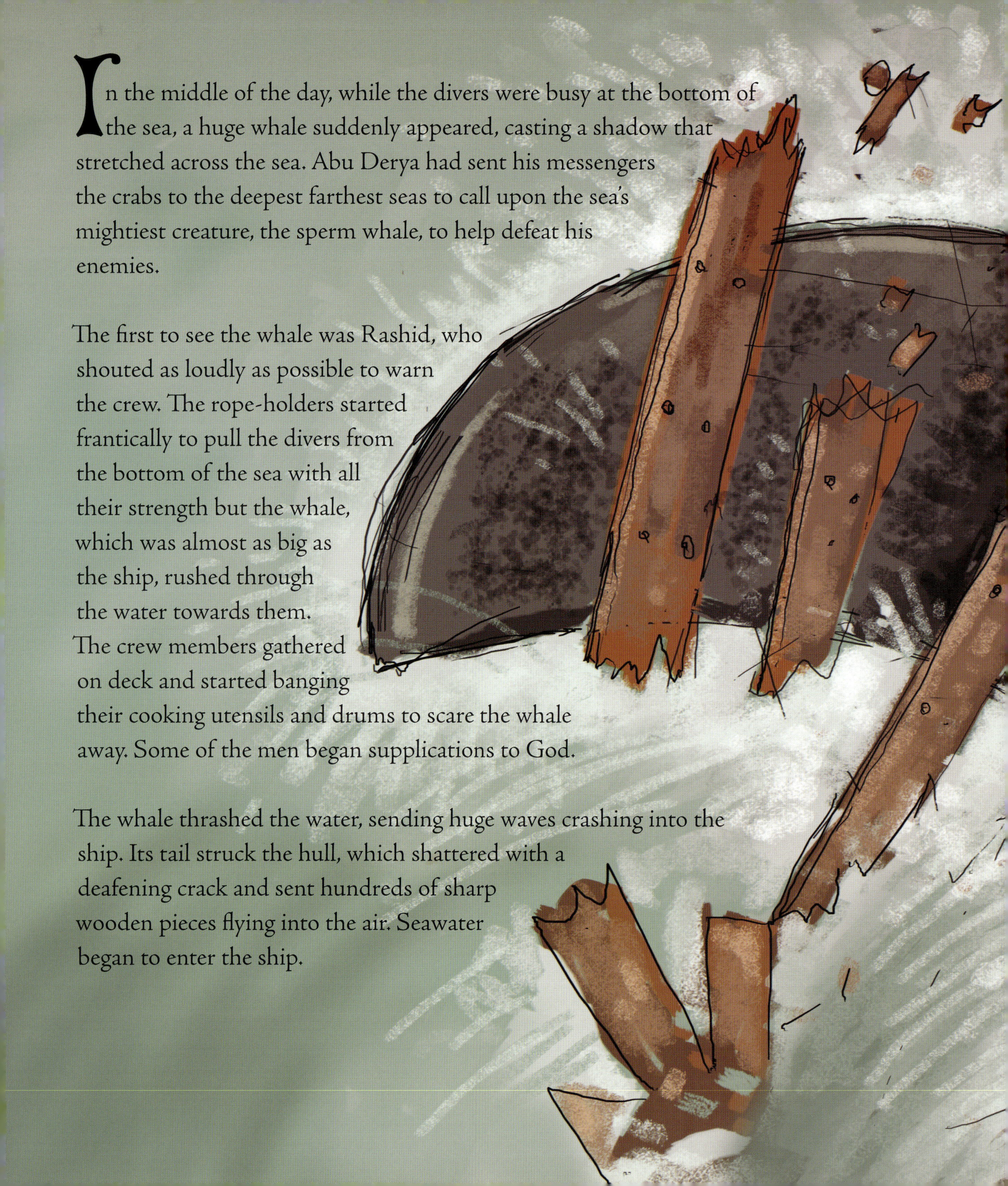

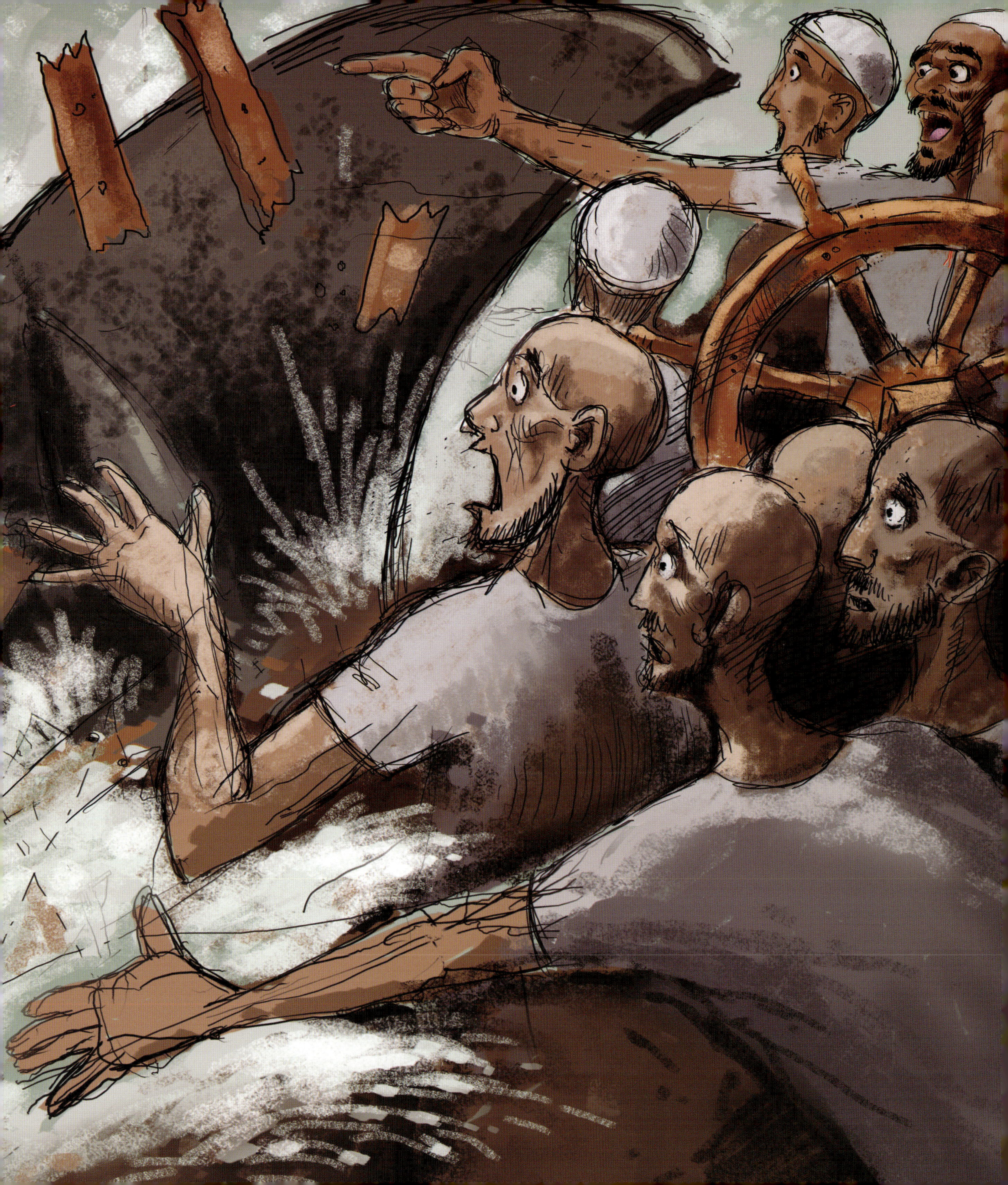

Firing a shot from the ship's cannon, the emir alerted the nearby boats of the danger. At the sound of the cannon the whale took fright and retreated, leaving the damaged ship behind it.

As soon as the sailors in the nearby ships heard the shot they hurried to help. Working together, they managed to repair the damage caused by the whale and save the ship from sinking.

Abu Derya's spies, the crabs who were following the ships, reported what had happened. Abu Derya was sitting on an ancient wreck when he heard that the whale's attack had failed, that the damages were slight and that the sailors had resumed their diving.

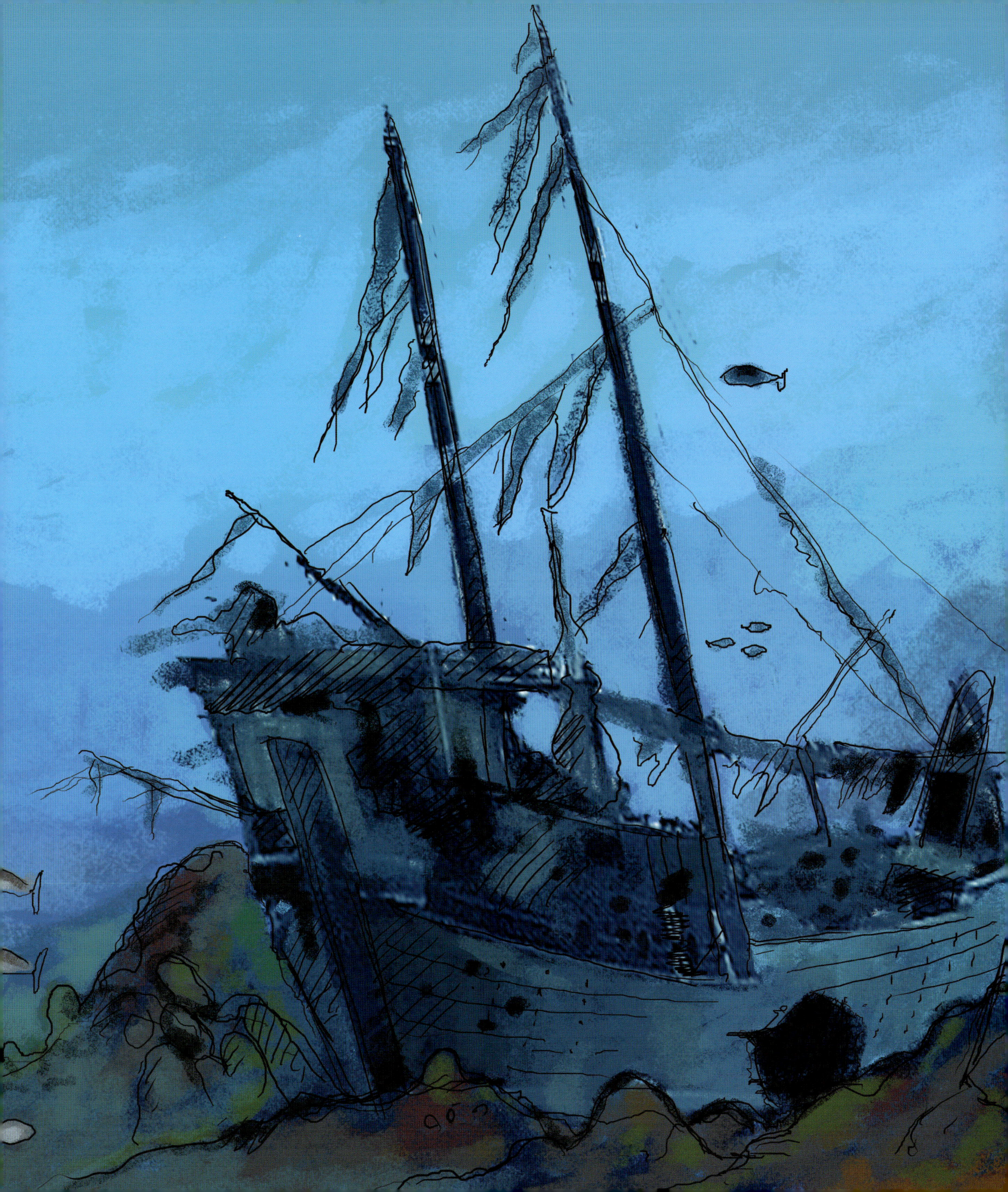

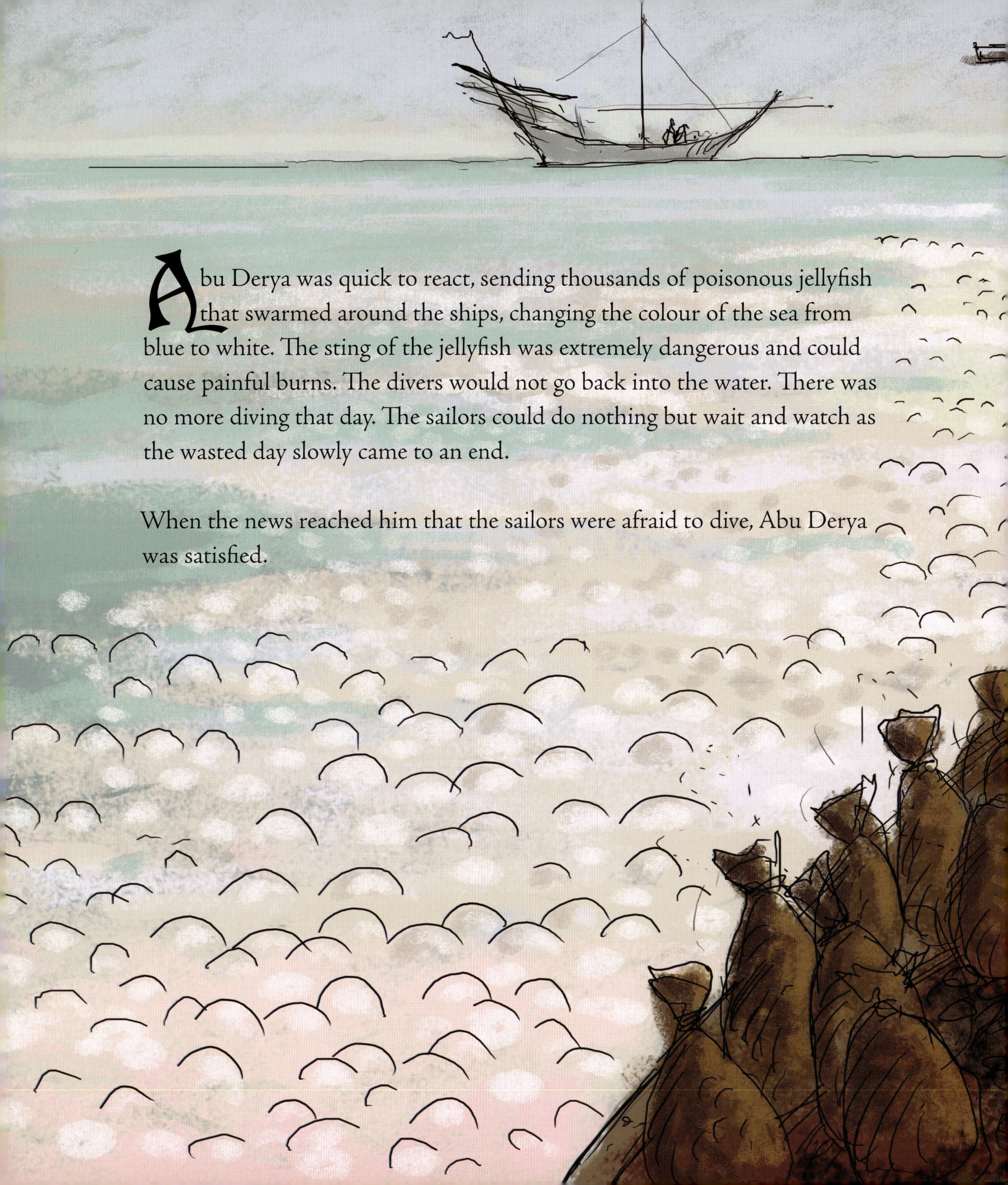

Abu Derya was quick to react, sending thousands of poisonous jellyfish that swarmed around the ships, changing the colour of the sea from blue to white. The sting of the jellyfish was extremely dangerous and could cause painful burns. The divers would not go back into the water. There was no more diving that day. The sailors could do nothing but wait and watch as the wasted day slowly came to an end.

When the news reached him that the sailors were afraid to dive, Abu Derya was satisfied.

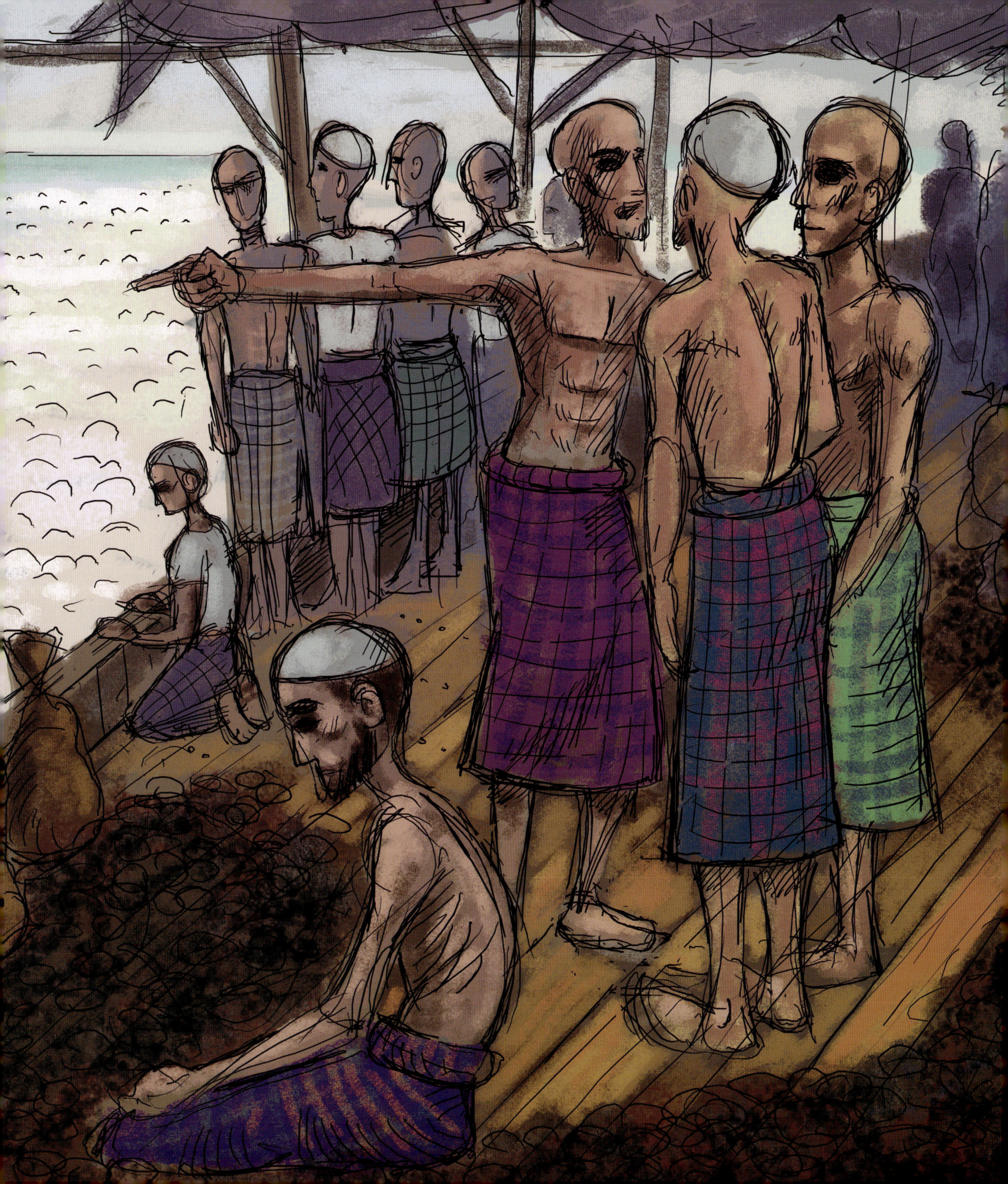

After the evening prayer the sailors surrendered to sleep. During the night the ships began to rock violently from side to side. The wind howled as the raging waves crashed against them. The sailors were terrified that they would be thrown into the sea. Was this Abu Derya's victory cry?

Just before dawn the wind grew calm. As the muezzin called the dawn prayer the waves died down, the sea became quiet and the ships were still.

The sailors performed their prayers. While they drank their morning coffee and ate the dates the sky was lit by the sun's rays, bringing a welcome surprise. The colour of the sky had changed to pure blue and the jellyfish had disappeared. The sailors could not believe their eyes. The storm had driven away the jellyfish and they could continue to dive.

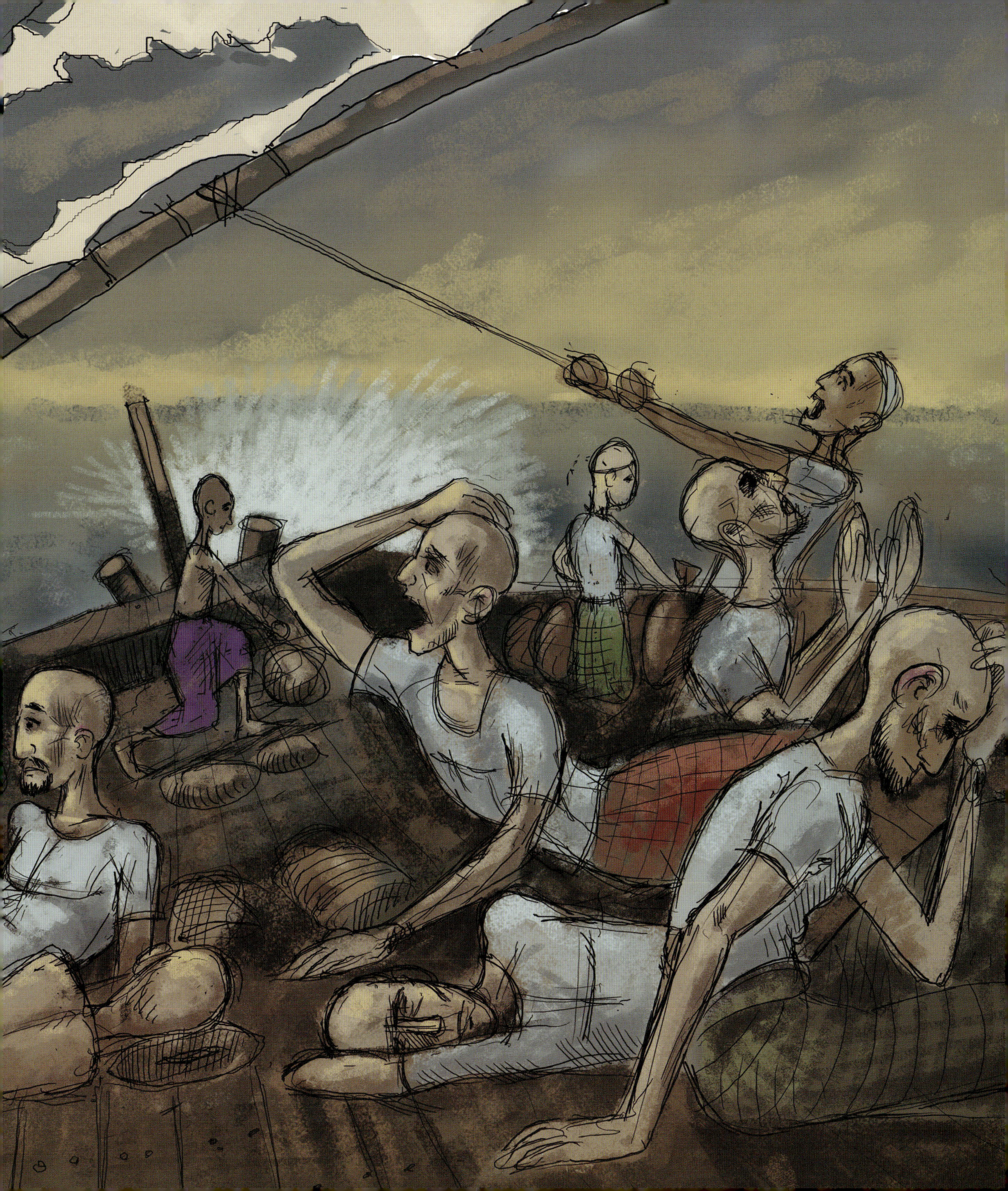

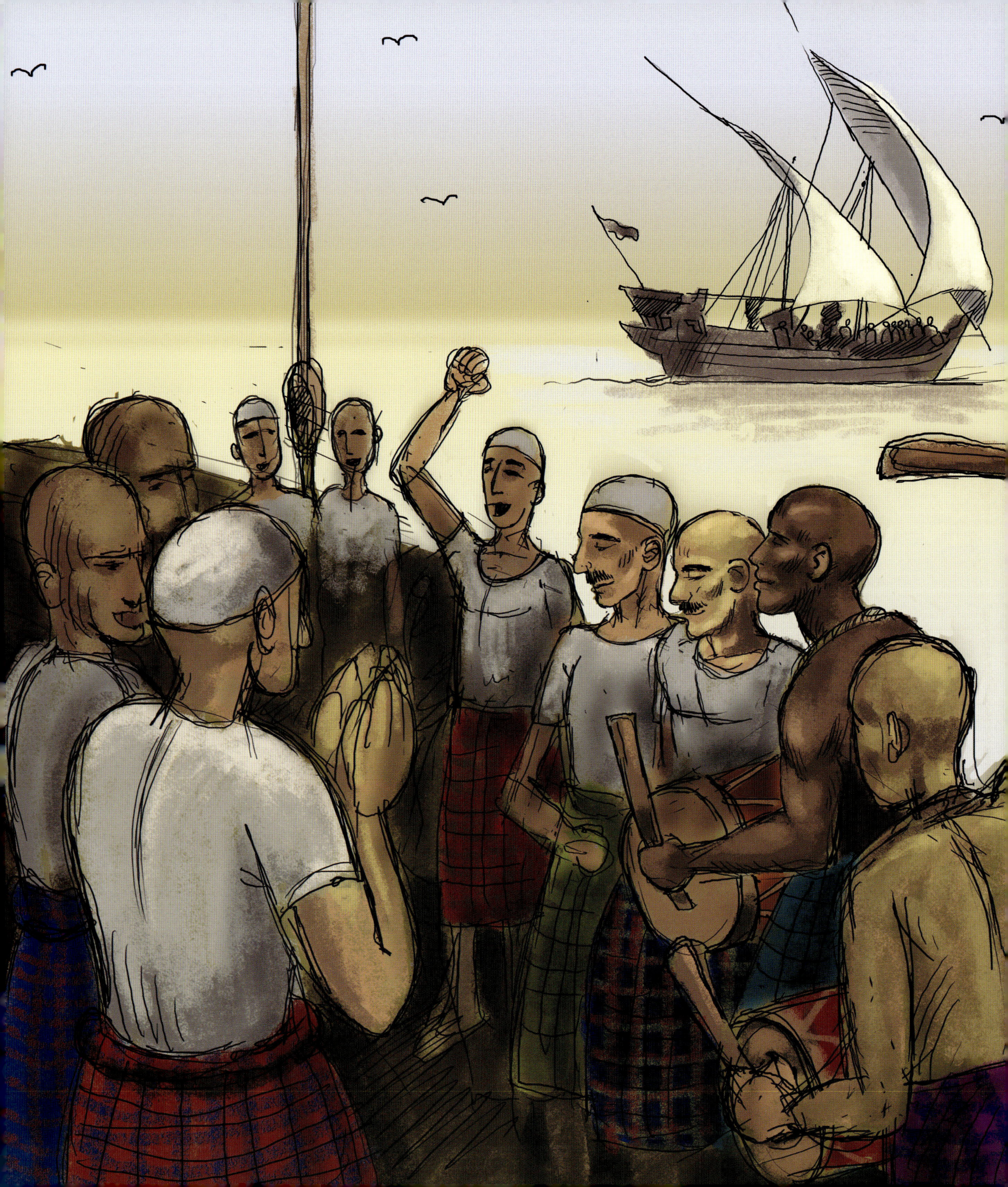

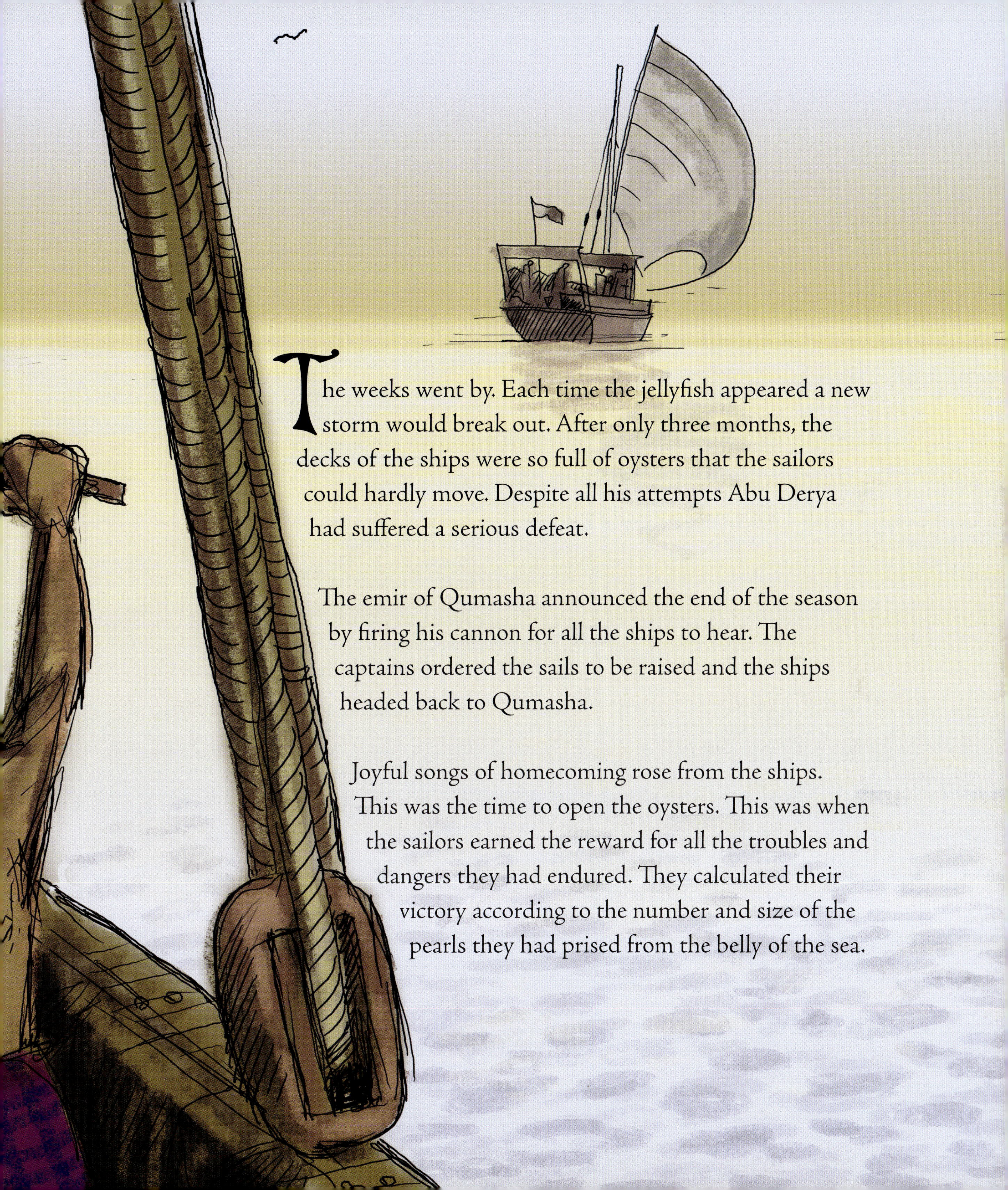

The weeks went by. Each time the jellyfish appeared a new storm would break out. After only three months, the decks of the ships were so full of oysters that the sailors could hardly move. Despite all his attempts Abu Derya had suffered a serious defeat.

The emir of Qumasha announced the end of the season by firing his cannon for all the ships to hear. The captains ordered the sails to be raised and the ships headed back to Qumasha.

Joyful songs of homecoming rose from the ships. This was the time to open the oysters. This was when the sailors earned the reward for all the troubles and dangers they had endured. They calculated their victory according to the number and size of the pearls they had prised from the belly of the sea.

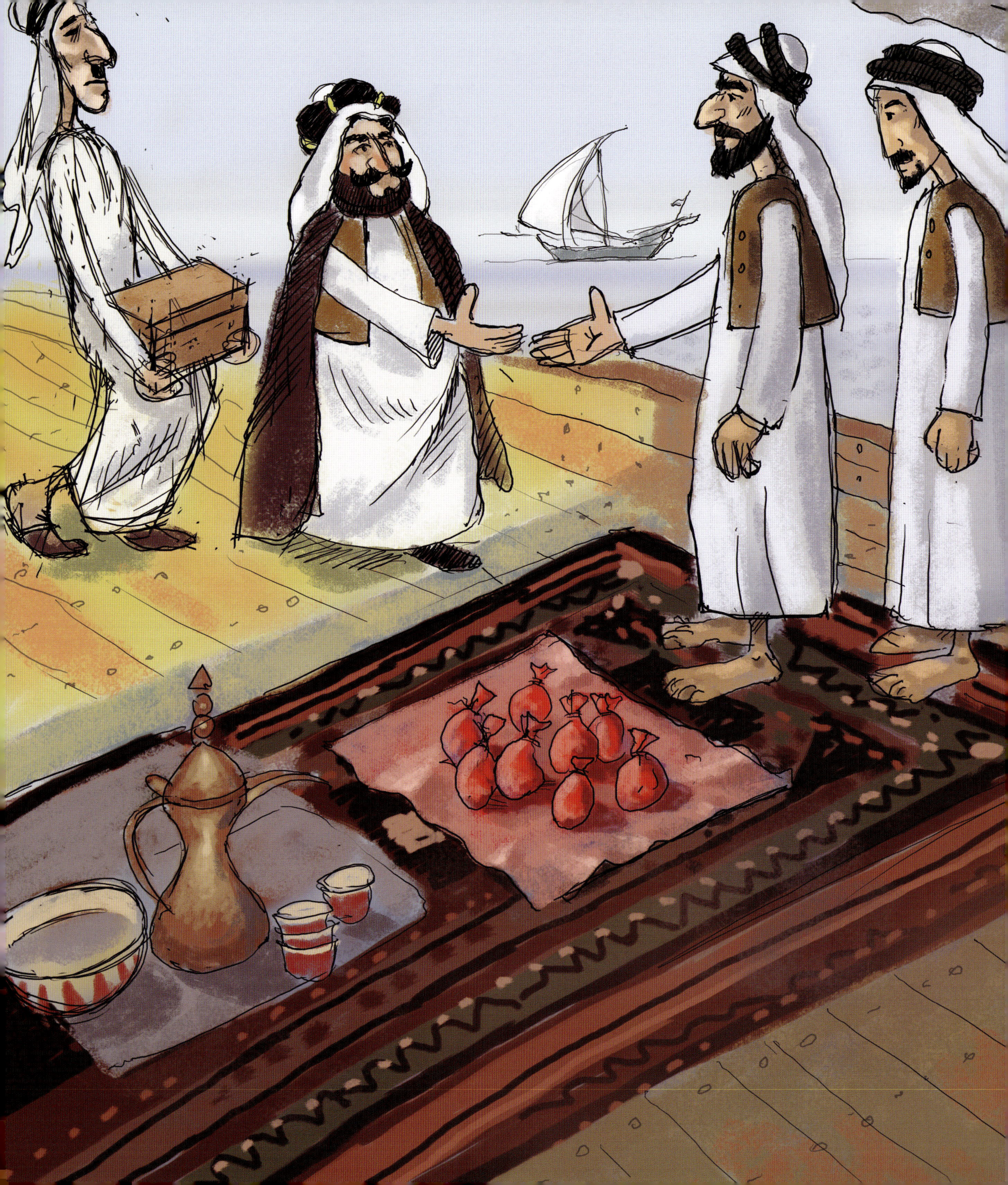

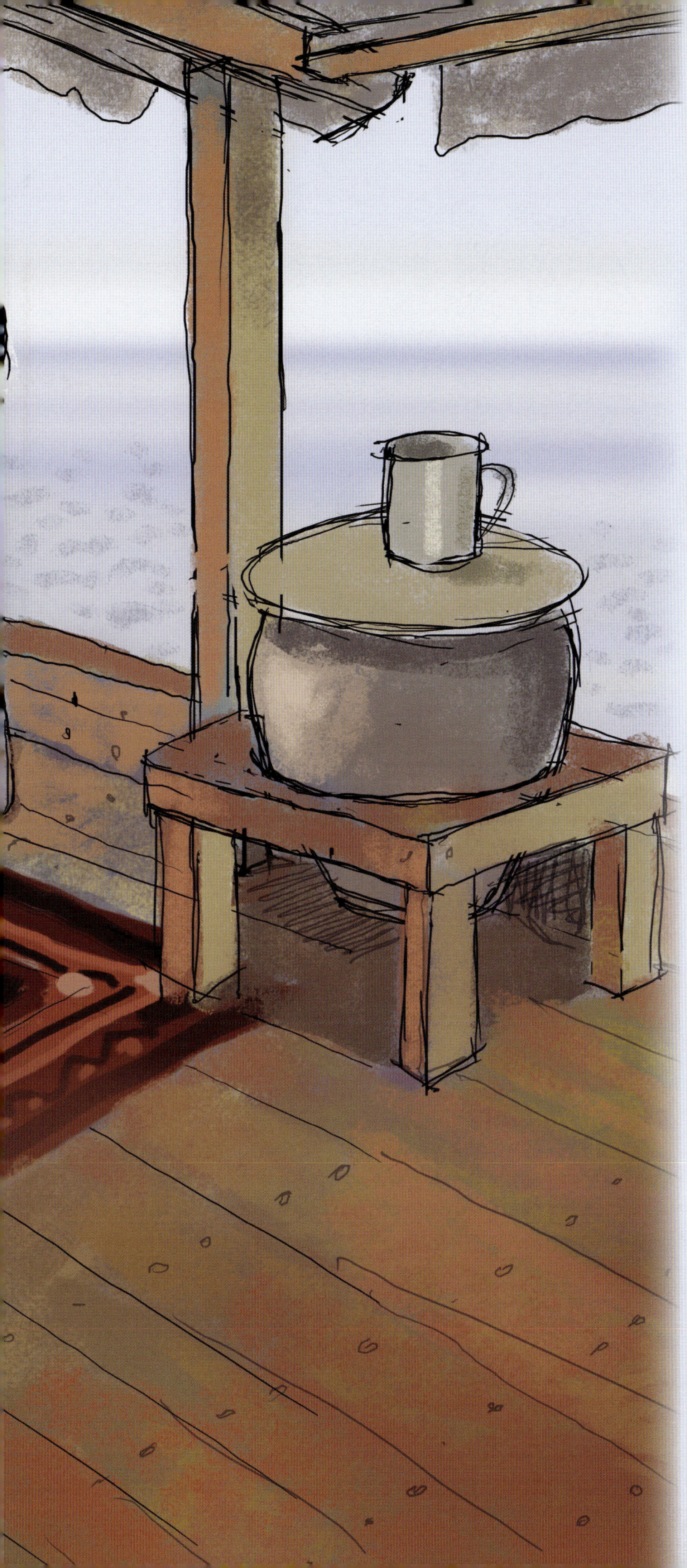

Before the ships had reached the shore, the ships of the pearl traders arrived alongside.

The ship of the trader Ahmed bin Sultan approached the ship of the emir of Qumasha. The captain lowered the sail and dropped the anchor into the sea. The sailors of the two ships exchanged greetings. The trader went on board the emir's ship, followed by one of his servants carrying the cash chest. The captain prepared the pearls that they had extracted from the oysters. The pearls were kept inside red cloth pouches, each pouch containing pearls that were of the same type, colour and quality.

The first mate went to the front of the ship and raised a black flag to indicate to other traders that the ship was busy trading. After an hour of negotiations the trader returned to his ship followed by his servant with the cash chest, his face beaming at the deal he had concluded. Today he had bought pearls that he could sell for twice the price.

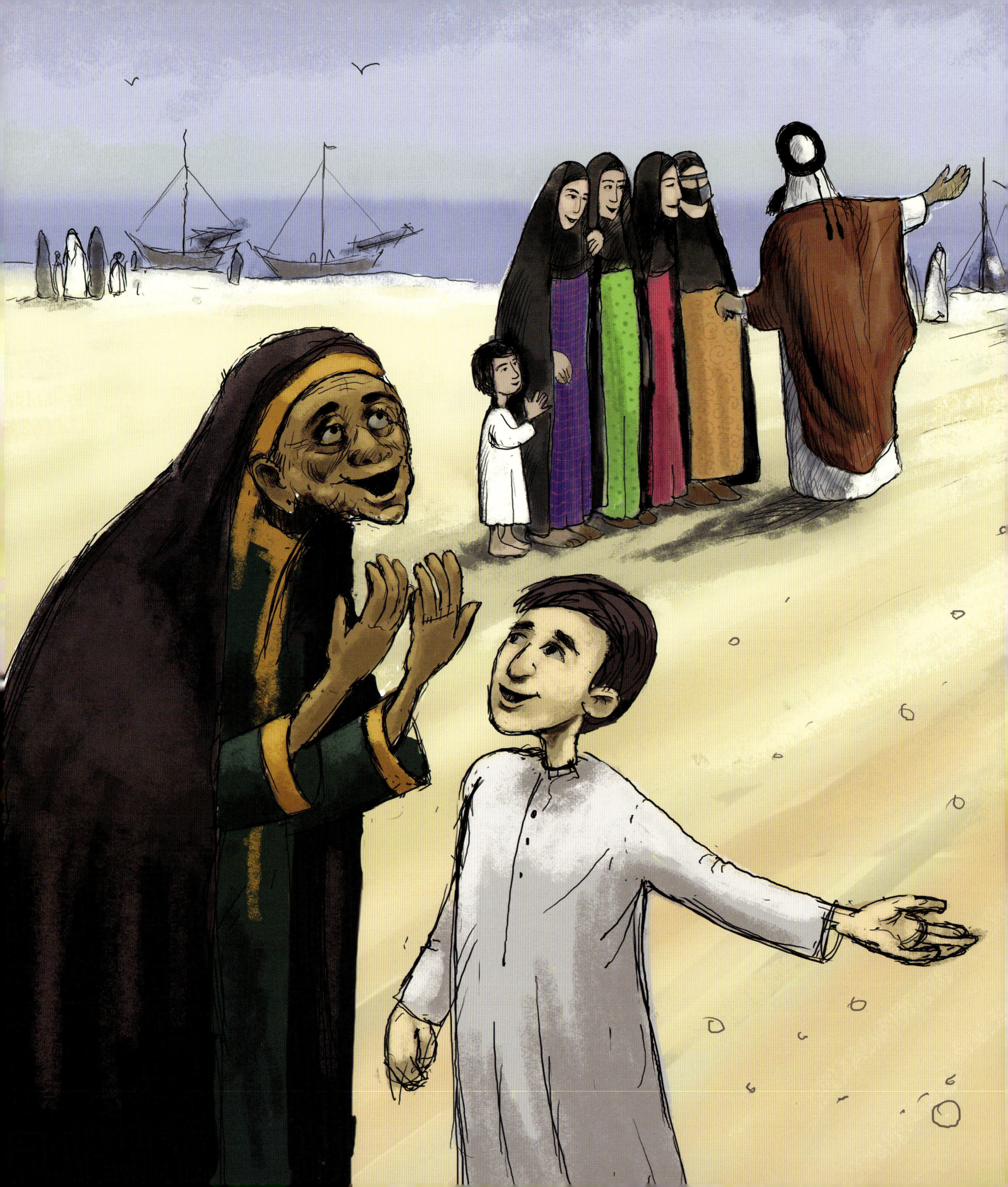

The ships returned to Qumasha with their sails raised in victory. The season had been a great one.

The people of the village prepared themselves to receive the men. The news had reached them of the victory over Abu Derya. They had made a great profit this season, which would compensate for the losses of the previous year. All their ships were coming back safely and all their men were returning to their families.

The men's desire to reach the shore was so great that they used the oars to speed the ships back to the village they had missed so much. After a three-month absence, one after another, the ships reached the shore. The sailors disembarked, greeting their families and embracing their children.

When Rashid came ashore his grandmother was waiting. She lifted her hands to the heavens. "This year God has blessed the village of Qumasha," she said. Then she turned to Rashid and added, "May your presence bring blessings to every voyage."

"It was your dream that came true, grandmother," replied Rashid. "You helped us to defeat Abu Derya!"

# The world of the pearl divers

## Who would you find?

**al Serdaal:** The emir of the fleet, appointed by the village to lead the expedition

**al Nokhadha:** The captain of the ship, with knowledge of the best oyster beds

**al Muqaddimi:** The first mate, or second-in-command

**al Seeb:** The man who monitored the rope between the diver and the ship, and pulled the diver up to the surface

**al Radeef:** The young apprentice who was training to become a diver

**al Tabaaba:** The junior apprentice who was also a deck hand responsible for basic tasks such as making tea

**al Nahhaam:** The singer of the traditional pearling songs, who kept up the crew's morale

**al Tawaash:** The pearl trader

## What equipment did the divers use?

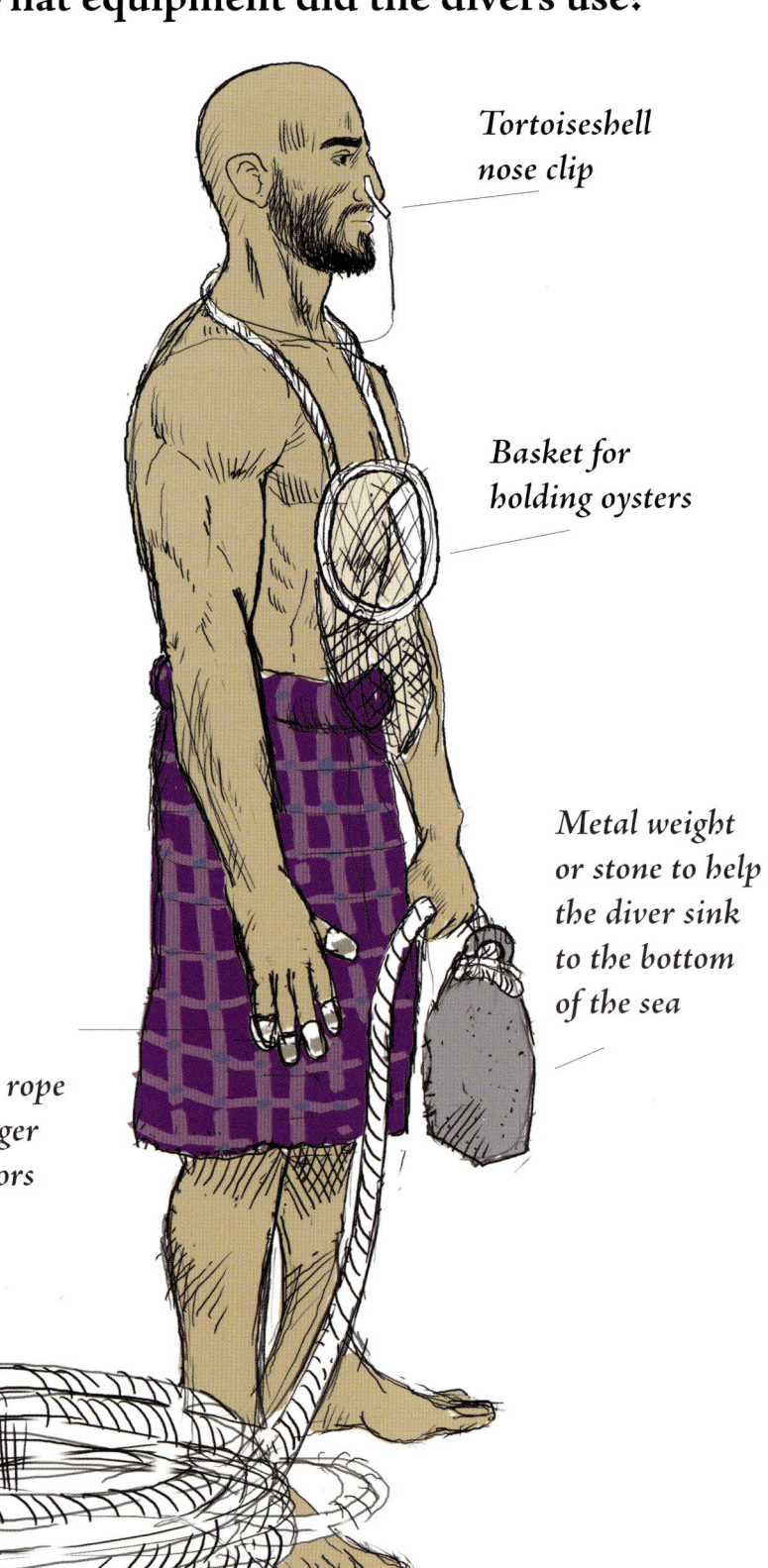

Tortoiseshell nose clip

Basket for holding oysters

Metal weight or stone to help the diver sink to the bottom of the sea

Diver's rope and finger protectors

# What kinds of ships did the pearl fishers use?

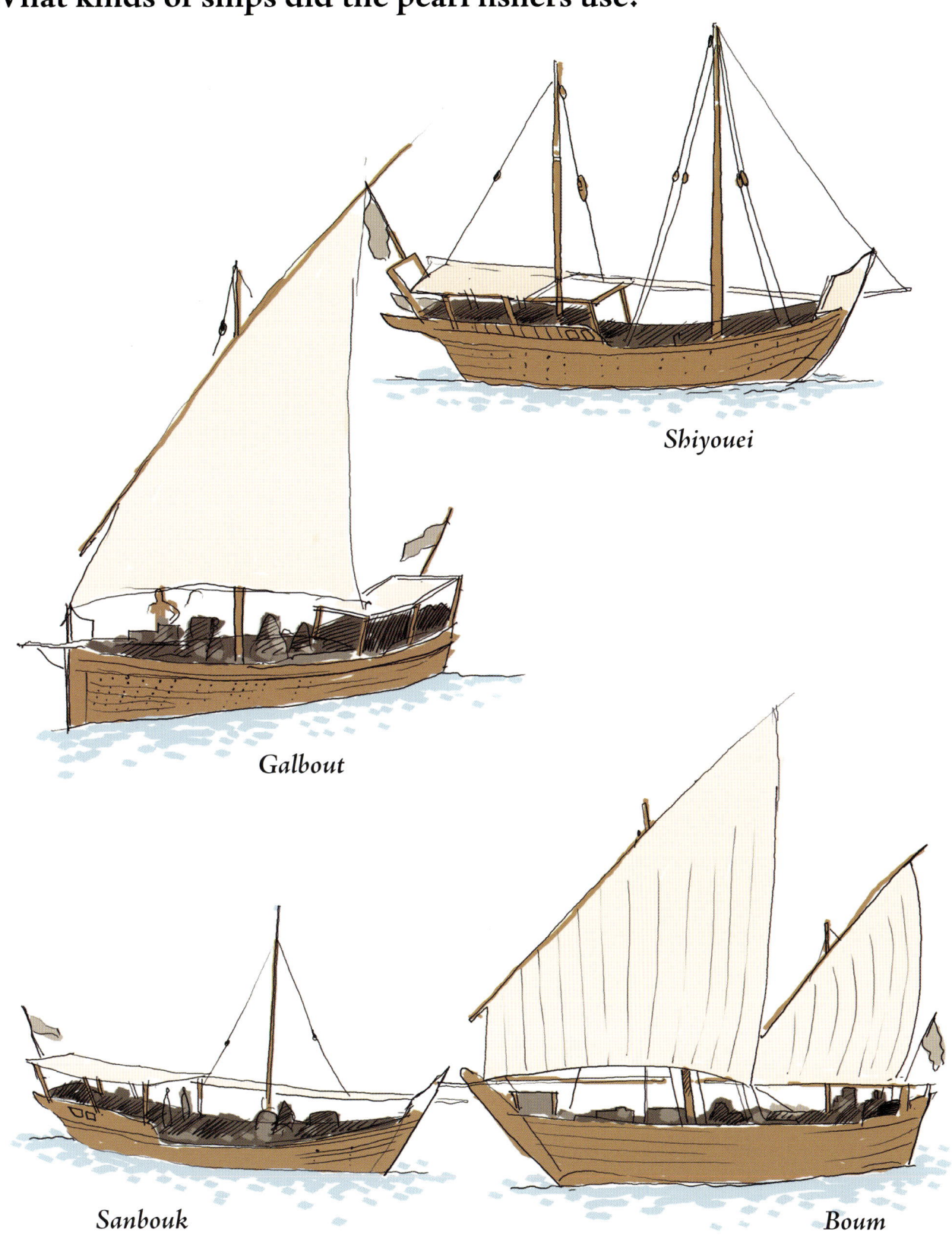

Shiyouei

Galbout

Sanbouk

Boum

*Mohammed Ali*

Mohammed Ali has authored and illustrated many children's books. He has also supervised national arts and heritage projects and has been involved in the research and documentation of the arts, crafts and architecture of the Gulf region.

In addition to writing children's books, Mohammed has also produced and presented children's programmes in Qatar and the Arab world.

He lives in Doha.

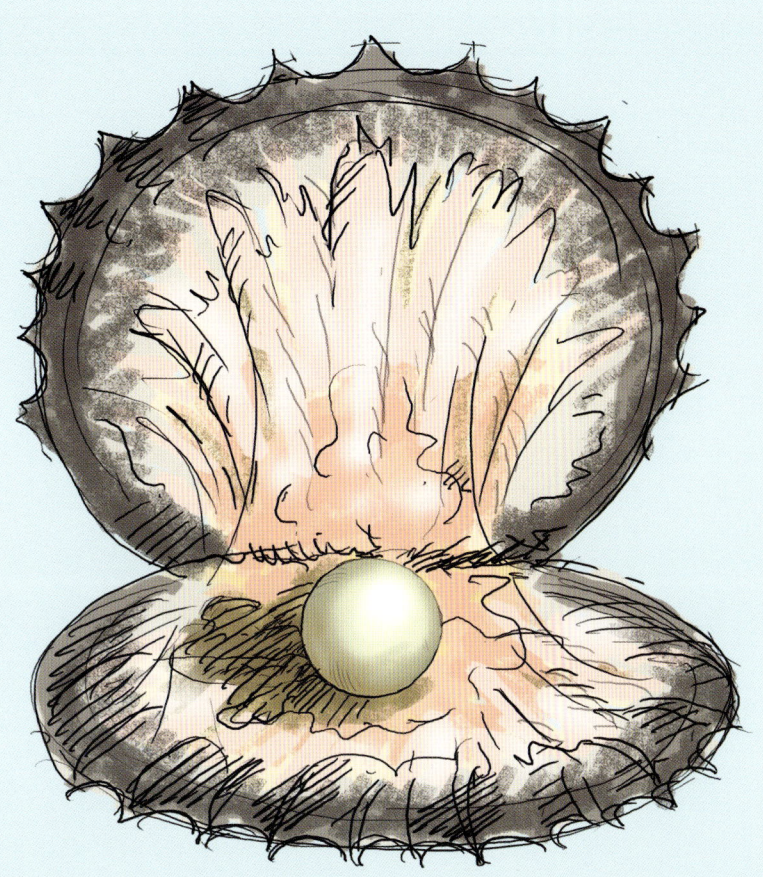

Victory Over Abu Derya: The Quest for Pearls in the Arabian Gulf
First published in 2010

Bloomsbury Qatar Foundation Publishing
Qatar Foundation
Villa 3, Education City
PO Box 5825
Doha, Qatar
www.bqfp.com.qa

Published in Association with Qatar Museums Authority

ISBN 9789992142233
99921-42-23-5
Cover by Ian Butterworth
Printed in the UAE


دار بلومزبري– مؤسسة قطر للنشر
BLOOMSBURY
QATAR FOUNDATION
PUBLISHING

مؤسسة قطر
Qatar Foundation

QATAR MUSEUMS AUTHORITY

متحف الفن الإسلامي
MUSEUM OF ISLAMIC ART
DOHA-QATAR

2010
Al-Doha Capital of Arab Culture

مركز التعليم
EDUCATION CENTRE
Culture of Learning